Calling the Griffin

A GREAT LAKES ADVENTURE
IN HISTORY & MYSTERY

by

Janie Lynn Panagopoulos

River Road Publications, Inc.
Spring Lake, Michigan

Jacket and book illustrations are by Don Ellens
The Panagopoulos drawing is by Carolyn Stich
Book design is by Patricia Westfield

ISBN: 0-938682-64-4

Copyright © 2001 by Janie Lynn Panagopoulos

Dedicated with respect and appreciation to my uncle, James Edson Critikos, and his wife, Shimako (Sue) Critikos

Contents

Special Thanks

A special thanks to John and Shelley Innis for the use of their sons' names, Lucas, Thomas, and Dimitirus Innis.

Also a special thanks to my friend Diana Lynn Hack for lending her name.

A Note from the Author

Although the French explorer La Salle really did lose his ship, the *Griffin*, on the Great Lakes and no trace of it has ever been found, *Calling the Griffin* is a fictional account of history and meant to be entertaining.

It is true, however, that the Great Lakes themselves hold many mysteries, many stories—and some of them are tragic ones. My hope is that you will be inspired to learn more about the lakes and the great history that surrounds them

Janie Lynn Panagopoulos
Mystorian (History + Mystery)

All collapsed, and the great shroud
of the sea rolled on as it had
five thousand years ago.

Herman Melville, *Moby Dick*

1

St. Joseph

"Mom, how long do we have to wait? It's hot out here."

"Allie, just be patient. The man said he would meet us at the fountain at 11:30."

Shoo peered down at his watch. Carefully balancing his ice cream cone he pushed the button on its digital face. "It's 11:35. He's late. Where is he?"

"Mom, it's hot. Can't we just go into someplace air-conditioned and let Dad and Shoo wait for the key?"

"No, we can't. Now just eat your ice cream cone and relax. Let's go sit in the shade, out of the sun."

Allie and her mom made their way to a green park bench that overlooked the sidewalk and street while Shoo and his father walked around a large white stone fountain filled with bubbling blue water. Shoo reached down into the water and splashed his hand around in it. His father frowned at him and shook his head.

"Allie, let me have a taste of your ice cream. It looks good," said her mother as she leaned back and put her arm across the back of the bench.

"See," said Allie as she handed her cone to her mother. "It is hot, isn't it? Be careful. The cone is dripping all over the place. I just love Mackinac Island Fudge ice cream, don't you?"

Allie's mother leaned forward so that the ice cream leaking from the cone would not drip onto her clothes.

"How will we know this man when he comes?"

"He said he would find us. He is an older

gentleman and lives in town now. According to your Aunt Diana, he owns the cottage next to hers at the beach."

"Is that why he has the keys to her cottage?"

"Yes, I suppose. And he's also her friend. He is the one who sold her the place." Mrs. Spywell took a large bite of ice cream.

Allie looked up and watched Shoo as he lapped his cone and read a large green metal marker that was near the road.

"Do you think Shoo is weird?" asked Allie wrinkling up her nose.

"Weird? Allie, that's not nice. What do you mean weird? He's your brother."

"I know. But boys, they are—well, you know—weird."

Just then Shoo stretched his arms over his head, holding his cone high into the air and wiggling his rear in a little dance. "Wow! Did you guys read this?" he hollered to them. "This is really cool."

Allie looked over to her mother, "See what I mean?" Allie scrunched up her face, and her mother started to laugh as she bit into the ice cream cone again.

"Mom! Don't eat all my ice cream!"

"Sorry. It's just so good."

"I know. I like it, too." Allie reached out and took the cone from her mother's hand, replacing it with a napkin. "Here. You're all gooey."

"Hey Allie!" yelled Shoo again, still standing next to the marker. "This place, right here, used to be a fort—**Fort Miami**."

"Miami's in Florida, you dingbat," Allie responded.

"FORT Miami. The marker says Fort Miami was here!"

Mr. Spywell joined his wife and daughter in the shade on the park bench. He stretched out his long legs and arms and yawned loudly. Allie looked at her mother and giggled. Weird, she thought.

"This used to be **Oumiamis**, or Miami Indian Territory before the **Iroquois** ran them out of Michigan a few hundred years ago," said Mr. Spywell.

"**La Salle**, the man who built the fort called this river the Miami River, and that is why the fort is named Fort Miami."

"The Miami River?" questioned Allie. "That's not its name now."

"They say Jesuit priests renamed it a few years after La Salle was here. The name St. Joseph River appeared on maps around 1700. About that time the French were getting a foothold in the Detroit area and French settlements were spreading throughout the Great Lakes.

"Did you know the French used to call the Mississippi River the Belle River or Ohio River because they thought it was all one long waterway from east to the west? They also thought that the Ohio River might be the **Northwest Passage** to the Orient."

"I learned about the Northwest Passage in school, but I didn't know they thought it was the Ohio River," commented Allie.

Not to be left out of the conversation Allie's mother added, "Did you know the French used to call Lake Michigan *Lac de Illinois* and the Indians called it *Machihiganing*? Kind of strange, isn't it? It's strange to think that all the names we use today, even the names of the Indian tribes, have been changed over the years."

Allie smiled and nodded as she listened. She was glad her father was an **archaeologist** and her mother was a writer, because they knew so many things.

Shoo darted over to join them on the bench. "Scoot over!" commanded Shoo to his sister. "Wasn't La Salle an explorer or something?"

"Ya, or something. Duh. . ." Allie said, rolling her eyes at Shoo.

"He was an explorer, and an interesting one at that," added Mrs. Spywell. "When I was in Canada last year doing research on that maritime project, I ran across a lot of material on him. He was quite the **entrepreneur**."

"En-tre-pren-manure?" asked Shoo.

"Not manure, you silly," said his mother with a chuckle.

"See what I mean, Mom, just weird," commented Allie.

"I am not!"

"An entrepreneur is a businessperson, Shoo. La Salle was a businessman during the fur trade in the 1600s. He came here from France and was commissioned by **Frontenac,** then Governor of New France, to explore the Mississippi and build forts."

"Was he a fur trader, too?" asked Shoo.

"Well, he wasn't supposed to be, but he traded and sold furs anyway. He made a lot of people in Montreal and Quebec mad at him."

"Dad, you've worked on an archaeological dig at a **fur depot** before, haven't you?" asked Allie.

"Yes, actually, up around **Georgian Bay**. La Salle was there, too, at a place called Little Current."

"He sure got around," said Shoo. "Hey, when is that old guy supposed to bring the key for Aunt Diana's place? He is already fifteen minutes late."

Mrs. Spywell looked down at her watch. "He will be here. He said on the phone he was walking to the farmer's market this morning and would bring the key with him. He said he'd meet us at the fountain."

"Are you sure this is the right fountain?" asked Allie.

"Yes, this is the fountain with the ladies on it, across from the hotel, near the Fort Miami marker. Yes, this is the right fountain. Now just be patient."

Shoo pushed up against his sister on the bench and she pushed back. "Knock it off, Shoo."

"I don't have enough room. You're just so gigantic there is no place for me to sit."

"Mom, did you hear what he said?" Allie stuck her nose up in the air and squinted her eyes at her little brother. "You're weird," she whispered just loudly enough for him to hear.

"I heard that."

"All right, you two," interrupted their mother. "Stop it. We don't have to spend a week together at the beach if you don't want to. Diana was nice enough to offer her place

x

since she wasn't going to use it this summer. But we don't have to stay if all you are going to do is fight. I have work to do while I'm here, so I will need some quiet writing time with no arguments. Understood?"

Shoo scooted over a little and gazed out towards the shore of the St. Joseph River. "Dad? Don't you think it's strange that that La Salle guy built a fort all the way up here? This seems so high and far away from the river."

"Well, that is true, Shoo, but remember this place was probably selected as a **lookout** point because it is high. And if you walk out to the edge of this area and look around, you'll see that there is only one side of the fort that would have to be defended against an attack because the rest of it butts up to the edge of the hill."

"I guess that makes sense." Shoo licked his fingers and hand as the ice cream ran down to his arm.

"Oh, stop that. Yuck."

"What? It's dripping!"

"You're gross." Allie scrunched up her face at her brother and stuck out her tongue.

Shoo, without thinking, reached out his ice cream cone and touched it to the end of Allie's nose, bursting out in laughter as a blob of mushy ice cream stuck there.

"Mom!" whined Allie. "Did you see what he did?"

Shoo jumped up from the bench. "There! Let's see if you can lick it off your nose."

"Mom! Look at my nose!"

Shoo jumped around and laughed as Allie crammed the rest of her cone into her mouth and shot off the bench after him.

"Sit down, you two. I think the man is coming. Will you please behave yourselves?"

said Mrs. Spywell.

"But Shoo put ice cream on my nose," complained Allie.

Shoo danced around in delight as he stuffed the rest of his cone into his mouth with one giant push.

Allie's mother dampened a napkin with her tongue and reached for Allie's nose.

"No!" she pushed her mother's hand away from her face. "I'll get it." Allie pulled the napkin from her mother's hand and folded it so it was dry on the outside. She wiped her nose off, casting an icy stare at her brother.

Shoo was paying no attention. He was looking down the sidewalk, staring at a bent, rumpled old man walking towards them. The old man had on baggy pants, a wrinkled plaid shirt with a blue sweater, and a cap.

Shoo wondered why the man needed a

sweater on such a warm day.

In his hand he carried a small white plastic sack. He looked like he had slept in his clothes, thought Allie, as he approached. When the man came closer, they both could also see he hadn't shaved in a while either.

Shoo sat down next to Allie who promptly elbowed him.

"Ow," she whispered.

"Shh," scolded their mother who sat up straight and stared at them with a threatening look in her eye.

"You think this is the guy?" whispered Allie to Shoo.

"I hope not," whispered Shoo. "He's scary looking."

Lucas Thomas Dimitrius

"You wouldn't be the Spywell family, would you?" asked the rumpled old man as he approached the bench. His voice was dry and crackly; he coughed and spit toward the edge of the sidewalk.

Allie stared at the man, her eyes growing wide as she watched him. Yuck, she thought.

Mr. Spywell grinned at his wife and nodded his head as he stood to address the stranger. "Yes sir, that we are." He extended his hand out in greeting to the old man.

Allie and Shoo watched as the man shifted his white plastic sack to his other hand and reached for their father's hand.

"I'm L.T. Dimitrius. Lucas Thomas

Dimitrius, that is."

"Pleased to meet you, sir. This is my wife and our two children, Allie and Sher. . ."

Shoo quickly jumped up from the bench and stood beside his father, not wanting him to tell the stranger his real name was Sherlock. Shoo offered his hand. "I'm Shoo."

"His name is Sherlock," Allie blurted out loudly.

"Pleased to make your acquaintance son, ma'am, miss. The old man tipped his cap a bit and than grabbed onto Shoo's hand like a vice and pinched down with a rapid shake. When he released Shoo's hand, he pulled away and rubbed his fingers together. "You got something sticky on your hand, son."

Embarrassed, Shoo grinned. "Sorry, it's just ice cream."

Allie got up from the bench with her napkin and offered it to the old man.

"Allie, he doesn't want that. Mom spit on it, and you wiped your nose on it."

"Shoo!" snapped his mother.

"It's all right, son," said the old man with a twinkle in his watery blue eyes. "I've had worse than ice cream on my hands before." The old man chuckled as he pulled a large, dingy-gray handkerchief out of his back pocket. It looked like it had been used to wipe worse than sticky fingers. Adjusting the plastic sack in his hand again, he wiped his fingers. "Got me a melon down at the farmer's market this morning. Cheaper than the store and a whole lot fresher. Got good melons around here this year," he commented. "If you would have gotten here a mite bit earlier, you might have been able to get yourself a bargain."

Shoo and Allie sat down beside their mother, who glared at them to behave.

"Yes," she said. "We will need to go to

the grocery store after we see what Diana has left at the cottage. She told us to eat up what was there so she wouldn't have to throw it away."

"Nice lady, that Diana. She hasn't been around much this season. I kind of miss seeing her pretty red hair," he said with a grin.

"All right then!" interrupted their father with a laugh. "So you have a key for us?"

"Sure do. Just let me get my rag back into my pocket here and I'll get it out." The old man crammed the dirty hankie back into his pocket, adjusted his bag, and patted both front pockets of his pants. "I know I got that key someplace. Unless I lost it on the walk down here."

Mrs. Spywell swallowed hard, hoping L. T. had not lost the key to Diana's cottage.

"Here we go, here we go." The old man crumpled up the bottom of his sweater feeling the pocket for the key. "It's right here. I forgot where I put it for a minute. Sign of a busy person, they say, when you forget where you put things."

The old man pulled a bright pink plastic ring with a brass key attached out of his pocket. "It'd be hard to lose that thing," he chuckled.

Mr. Spywell snickered. "That sure is bright pink, all right."

"Now you know where to find the place, don't you?"

"Well, I think I know the way," said Mrs. Spywell as she stood. "I know we just go back out of town and follow the shore about five miles."

"Well, yeah, you got the general direction right, but not far enough," interrupted the man. "Go on up here and follow the road out past all those old Victorian mansions they got out there. Keep going until you see a tall stand of cedars by the road. You'll pass the overlook and the bluff and then those cedar trees. Take a right down that road. It is only paved about 100 feet down there and the rest is dirt and sand. Keep following along down the shoreline and you'll see them standing there."

"See them?" asked Mr. Spywell.

"The houses. Two houses on a little knoll overlooking the water, up just a little off the shore. We have the only two places out there, Diana's and mine. Can't miss 'em. The first cottage is mine, not fancy, just forthright. Not quite as pretty as your friend's place anymore. It used to be though. Your friend's place looks like a dollhouse now. Even has **haint blue** shutters on it to keep the ghosts out."

"The ghosts?" asked their mother. "Excuse me, did you say ghosts?"

"You folks ain't afraid of any little old

ghosts are you?"

Allie and Shoo's eyes grew wide. They looked at one another, remembering their experience on Isle Royale.

"You don't mean ghosts, like. . ."

"I mean ghosts. The cottages are haunted. They won't hurt you none though. Been around those two places for over seventy years and I'm still here to talk about it, aren't I? Those cottages both used to belong to my people. The one your friend owns used to belong to my Uncle Lucas Thomas. Thomas is a family name. That's where I got my name. I was called Little Lucas after my uncle.

"The place that I still own was the one I was raised in by my mother. She's gone now. All of them are gone now. Ain't no one around anymore but me. Me and your friend, that is. The place just needed a little love and attention, and that is just what it got when Diana bought it. She sure has nice red hair, don't you think?"

Allie started to giggle, thinking that the old man must have a crush on their Aunt Diana.

"Well, Diana didn't say anything about her cottage being haunted," said their mother.

"She didn't tell you? What do you think she painted her shutters haint blue for? That's the old witchy trick. Spooks don't like that color so it helps to keep them out. Don't know what my old uncle would think about that, since it is his old place. Lived there all his life. He was a bachelor and fisherman. Used to fish these very waters for years. Why, he'd bring in his catch and gut and clean the fish out right there in the cottage before he'd take them on into market."

"He'd gut the fish in the cottage?" asked

their father.

"That's right. I told you he was an old bachelor just like me. No woman around to tell him what to do. He used to like to sit in there with the door wide open so he could see the lake and just clean and cut those fish into big tubs. That's what I'd smell when he used to visit—after he passed, that is. He'd visit quiet frequently before those haint blue shutters.

"I'd get a whiff of fish guts and blood, then the lights would kinda flick off-and-on. Used to happen before there was goin' to be a big storm. He probably did that 'cause he's trying to warn me. That's the way he lost his life, you know."

Shoo stood and moved closer to old L. T. Dimitrius, not wanting to miss anything he had to say about ghosts. Allie not wanting to be left out, pushed her way up under her mother's arm.

"Does it still smell like fish in there now?" asked Shoo.

"Don't think so anymore, not since those haint blue shutters. I used to live there, as a young man after I moved out from my mother's care. I found it a comfort knowing my uncle was so near, even though his body was never found. Kind of miss having him around nowadays."

"You miss a ghost?"

"Allie, shh," said her mother.

"Might be strange to say but, yes."

"They never found his body? Where did it go?"

"Shoo, that is none of your business," interrupted his father.

"No, no, that's all right. The boy is just curious. I'd like to know that myself. It was a day just like this, bright and clear. About sixty years ago now, I guess. I was just a young man, just a mite bit older than this lad here." The old man rubbed the top of Shoo's head with his wrinkled, rough hand and smiled down at him. L.T.'s soft blue eyes stared away out over the busy riverway as he remembered.

"Yep, a day just like this it was, hot with a hint of a storm in the air, and it was my uncle's birthday. My uncle was a commercial fisherman, and he taught me his trade seeing he had no children of his own. I worked with him on his boat since I was just a small lad. I remember it like it was yesterday.

"That morning, before we went out, I gave him a gift of a red cap for his birthday. I had saved my money up for a long time to buy him that cap. It was bright red, real bright red. I got it that color so that I would be able to see him from shore if I wasn't on his boat with him. I wanted to be able to see if it was him from a long way off. My mother was alive then and she saved up her money and bought the fixin's to bake him a cake.

"My uncle was her brother, and he'd never had a birthday cake before."

"He never had a birthday cake before?" asked Shoo who looked over at Allie in disbelief.

"Yep, that's right, never had. My mother always promised to make him one, and this was the year. It was in the middle of the **Depression** and money was scarce. My father was away at the time, workin' in Chicago. We stayed here, my mother and I, and my uncle helped to look after us. He was a good man.

"Well, anyway, my uncle put on that bright red cap and was lookin' forward to that birthday cake of his.

"We put into the lake early so we could haul our catch and get home to that cake.

Otherwise it was the same routine as every other morning. Getting geared up in our **oilskins**. Making sure the tubs were empty and the bait trays were full and nets were straight on the wench for the drop. A day like any other day. We had no idea what that old lake had in store for us.

"I remember passing by the cottage on our way out into the lake and seeing my mother on the knoll waving good-bye to us—her white apron and red hair blowin' in the wind. She had no idea it would be the last time she would ever see her brother, no idea what fear was about to overcome her.

"The gulls followed us out wanting a free handout of fish. It sure was a pretty sight. We made our way north past the River St. Joe and then west towards deep water. All was unusually calm on the *Griffin* that morning, all the way to midday, that is.

"The *Griffin*, that was the name of Uncle Lucas's boat. He named it after La Salle's ship the *Griffin* that was lost on the Great Lakes a long time ago. Pretty fateful name, now that I think on it.

"Well, Uncle Lucas kept an eye on the barometer all morning. When it started to fall and dirty little clouds began forming in the northwest, we got an inkling something was coming in. The *Griffin* had a good running engine so there wasn't anything to fear. Never had a problem with her before, and we weren't expectin' one then.

"But then mighty fast the clouds started turning inside out and the sky looked like a heavy gray blanket with holes punched in it and fingers of light streaming through them. We decided it was time to make for shore. We pulled in the nets and secured them as best we could. It didn't take long for the wind to pick up after that, lifting the waves and layering them over with foam. Then the little foamy white caps broke into a churning boiling mess. The wind howled down and rocked the *Griffin* on the waves. It threw us around in the pilothouse like we were toys.

Then the engine started to give us trouble. The foam was spitting yellow because of the wind. We were losing power because there was more foam than water for the propeller to catch on to.

"Uncle Lucas pointed us into the waves. A wave, if higher than the ship, can flip ya end-over-end, if ya don't ride it right. Ya got to climb a wave at a 45-degree angle and slide down her other side. Uncle Lucas positioned us into the seas and we were hoping to ride with the storm.

"We were fine until the engine went down—burned out its bearings in the foam. There was nothing more we could do 'cept

watch the waves grow into gray angry mountains. That was when my uncle went out to loosen the lifeboat. He said it was getting to look like we might be needin' it.

"He was right. He insisted I stay in the pilothouse, as it was just too wicked out on **deck**. I watched through sheets of rain that hammered violently at the windows. I'll never forget it. All I could see was that bright red cap crammed down on his head, out there in that downpour. I watched that red cap closely. It was there one minute and the next it was gone, and so was Uncle Lucas."

Shoo listened intently to the story. He watched as L.T.'s face softened and tears, one after the other, escaped the rim of his eyes and caught in his scrubby beard.

Allie looked away. What a sad story, she thought. Poor L.T. Poor Uncle Lucas.

Mr. Spywell cleared his throat and asked.

"So your uncle drowned?"

"Yep, that's about the sum of it."

Mrs. Spywell asked softly, "L.T., how did you survive? That would have been an awful experience for a young man."

"That it was. That it was. I stayed with the *Griffin* until she started to rock so violently that I knew it was only a matter of time before she would roll.

"I mustered up all the courage I could to pull open the door of the pilothouse. I held onto anything I could get a hold of and fought the wind across the deck. Uncle Lucas had managed to loosen the lifeboat before he disappeared, and I crawled into it up under the **oilcloth** cover. I lay on the floor of that tiny boat and cried and prayed. I took the gutting knife I had in my pocket and drove it hard into the bench seat to serve as a handle to hold on to. I was at the mercy of the lake and I knew it.

"I have no idea how long I was in that **skiff**. It had to be just a matter of minutes when I felt the *Griffin* starting to pitch to the side. The skiff slid across the deck and caught up in the nets. It was a good thing for those nets. When the ship began to roll they flew out over the deck and pulled me along with them into the sea and away from the suction of the sinking *Griffin*. I could hear the ship creak and moan over the howling wind, then the sucking noise. It still haunts me to this very day."

"Who rescued you?" questioned Shoo, his eyes staring wide in amazement.

"Rescue? There weren't no rescuing. That storm there was the Storm of the Age, they called it. They found me the next morning, washed up on shore down south of here. It seems I rode the storm out in that lifeboat. It was that oilcloth cover that kept the seas out and me from sinking, driving me in front of the waves to land. They found me face down on the beach about frozen stiff and the skiff, all broken to splinters, just up the shore from me. Almost drowned that day, just like Uncle Lucas. Still carry the chill from that lake. Never been able to warm up since." L.T. pulled his sweater up around him.

"Mr. Dimitrius, you were lucky to have survived!"

"Yep, Mrs. Spywell, you're right. Ain't no one got no idea how I made it through, but I did."

"My poor mother though, she had given us both up for dead. She heard the church bells ringing, which meant trouble on the open water. People used to say if the men weren't home safe off the water by dawn, it was time to order the coffins. It wasn't until late in the evening the next day when they were able to get me a ride back home to her. She thought we both were gone."

"Why didn't they just call her on the phone to let her know you were safe?" wondered Allie.

"We didn't have a phone out there at the time. Couldn't afford it. Not many could. But I know when I was out on my own after that, I put a phone out there for just that reason. There still isn't a phone out there at Diana's place though. I keep warning her that she will never know when she might need it.

"My mother's hair, that poor woman, which was a pretty red like your aunt's, turned snow white that night because of the shock. She kept it white until the day she died as a testament of her fear of that lake. It got the best of her."

"I've heard of that happening," commented Mr. Spywell "but I never knew anybody that it had happened to."

"Well, sir, you do now. It's no wonder she wanted to leave that cottage after that. For the rest of her life she always wanted to move away but never did. My father didn't return from Chicago that fall, and no one ever heard from him again, either. Day after day, year after year, my mother lived down there, the lake pounding on the shore and the blasted sand blowing everywhere. Mercy, she hated that sand in the house. And the wind on stormy nights would paralyze her with fear. She would just sit all night wrapped up in a blanket and rock back-and-forth, back-and-forth before the fireplace, waiting for the church bells to ring, waiting for the storm to go away.

"I think it drove her mad. Perhaps I'm a little mad too, no telling." L.T. chuckled to himself.

"I don't spend much time down there at the cottage anymore, and I never spend the night. Now that I'm getting older it holds too many bad memories. The pounding of that old lake has lost it charm for me."

Allie put her arm around her mother and thought about L.T.'s experience.

"They never found your uncle's body?" asked Mr. Spywell.

"From that lake? Sometimes a lake is like a mother—she has her favorites and won't let them go. That's what I like to think. Uncle Lucas loved the *Griffin* and he loved this old lake. It appears the lake, she loved him, too.

"The people of the town walked the beach for a few days, kept fires lit down there watching, looking for anything that would wash up. I always hoped that red cap of my uncle's would come back to me, sort of as a sign he was all right there on the other side, but it never did.

"Uncle Lucas and the *Griffin* weren't the

only ones that were lost that day, either. I remember watching the shore for a long time for a bit of sail, oilskins, or anything that didn't belong there—even the body of a dead man. Wasn't much that returned from that storm, the Storm of the Age.

"My mother never cut into Uncle Lucas's birthday cake. She never ate a bit of it. She sent it up to the church where they had hot coffee and nourishment for those out walking the beach, looking for the dead. I remember takin' that cake up to the church and how quiet the women were when I brought it into them. Some of the men refused to eat any because they thought it had a curse on it.

"I remember I ate a bite of it. It was soft and sweet and washed down good with hot coffee. I know Uncle Lucas would have appreciated that birthday cake too."

"That's really a sad story, Mr.

Dimitrius."

"Yep, girl, that it is. Sad but true, every last bit of it. There are lots of sad stories and there are a lot of ghosts out on that lake and walkin' along the shoreline. That's why your friend there, Diana, painted the shutters haint blue, to keep the ghosts where they belong and not in her house. She did that after I told her the stories."

"Do you have ghosts at your house?" asked Shoo.

"Shoo!"

"That's all right for the boy to ask. Yes, son, lots of ghosts everywhere. I've never seen one, but I know when I am out there by myself and a storm starts to blow in and I smell the smell of fresh fish, it's my uncle letting me know he is still around lookin' after me like he did the day of the storm. Sometimes I even think I smell a cake bakin'. Or the drafts of air leak in around the old window near the fireplace and make my mother's rocking chair sway just a little. Funny how having a frightening experience makes you aware, makes you sense things of another world."

Allie and Shoo gazed at one another and wondered what it was going to be like to stay in a place that had known so much sadness.

"Well, I hate to leave good company," said Mr. Dimitrius as he pulled out his hankie and blew his nose. "It's getting late and I have to hike back to my place."

"Can we drop you off?" asked their father.

"No, the exercise is good for my old bones. I might even drop by my cottage later this afternoon, if I feel up to it. Last time I was there, I thought I heard some squirrels up in the attic and the lights kept blinking on and off. Probably chewed their way through the insulation. I wouldn't be surprised if I found a **carcass** or two up there because of it. Got to check it out before I have a fire."

"You said there was a grocery store not too far from the cottage?" asked Mrs. Spywell, trying to change the subject.

"Not far at all. Opened by newcomers about thirty years ago. Just about eight miles up from the cottage road. You'll pass it on the way down there.

"Don't forget your key now." L.T. dangled the bright pink key ring out to their mother.

"Well, it has been a pleasure, sir," said their father. "And thank you for sharing your story."

"Pleasure's all mine. I might drop by for a visit before ya leave. Enjoy the cottage and you two children beware of the beach and stay back from the water, no matter how calm and gentle she looks, she can be a danger."

Shoo and Allie nodded their heads.

The children watched as the old man, stooped with age and carrying the white sack with his melon in it, turned and walked slowly down the sidewalk.

"Come on," said their father. "We better go find this haunted cottage before it gets too late to enjoy the day."

The four turned and silently walked to their van.

Great Lakes Triangle

"Does L.T. mean," asked Allie, "that we can't go swimming while we're here? Is it that dangerous down at the lake?"

"I wanted to go swimming," said Shoo disappointedly. "I even brought my new kick-board."

"Well, I know you two aren't going swimming alone," said their father. "I just think Mr. Dimitrius doesn't like the water too much anymore. They're not on very good terms, he and that lake."

"We know that," commented Allie. "Do you blame him?"

"I think we need to see what the beach looks like and how deep the water is up by shore," added their mother.

"Yeah, but I wanted to use my kick-board."

"It doesn't matter what you want to do. Safety first. You know that."

"Yeah, I know," remarked Shoo grimly.

"Do you really think Mr. Dimitrius's uncle. . ."

"Uncle Lucas," Allie interrupted Shoo.

"Yeah, Uncle Lucas. Do you really think he died like L.T. said?"

"Well, I don't think Mr. Dimitrius would lie about something like that," said their father. "And a lot of strange things do happen on the Great Lakes. When I was in college I did a whole study about the myths and legends of the Great Lakes. There are ancient Indian stories about giant lizards and serpents with long tails that whip the Lakes into raging **whirlpools**, and evil spirits and demons reaching up with the fingers of the lake and stealing sailors right off the decks of their ships."

"Yes," added their mother. "I even heard, when I was working on that maritime project last year, about a Great Lakes Triangle."

"I remember reading about that, too," added their father.

"A Great Lakes Triangle? What is that?" questioned Shoo.

"I bet it's like the Bermuda Triangle!" blurted Allie.

"Yeah, right. What's that?"

Allie laughed. "You've never heard of the Bermuda Triangle? Where have you been?" Shoo scrunched up his shoulders, not knowing what they were talking about.

"It's this place in the Atlantic Ocean, by Bermuda and Florida, where tons of ships and airplanes disappear and strange storms happen all the time. Some people even think it's like a doorway into another dimension of time, a time **vortex** or something like that."

"No way, Allie, you're just making that up."

"No, I'm not. Am I, Dad? Mom, tell him I'm not making that up."

"No way. So you think that maybe the Great Lakes has something like a doorway to another time dimension? Cool! No wonder there are so many ghosts!"

"No, no, no, Shoo, we didn't say that at all," interrupted his mother. "And it's not just your father and I who know about this Great Lakes Triangle. There has been a lot of research done on the Great Lakes over the years, and there are some people who believe there really is something strange going on out there. Something like what happens near Bermuda that causes so many shipwrecks. Sometimes ships and aircraft just disappear and no one ever hears from them or sees them again."

"Like Uncle Lucas and his red cap," added Shoo.

"Well, not quite. He obviously drowned in the storm," commented his father.

"But how do you know? L.T. said he just disappeared off the deck of the boat. He was there one minute with his red cap and the next, he was gone. Maybe he just got swallowed up in a time dimension."

"Shoo, the man was swept overboard in a bad storm," insisted his mother.

"Yeah, Shoo. They called it the Storm of the Age like L.T. said," added his sister.

"You mean as Mr. Dimitrius said," corrected their mother.

"Like Mr. Dimitrius said."

"When I worked on the project in Canada, I learned that nowhere on earth are there freshwater seas as large as the five combined Great Lakes. The shorelines of

Lakes Huron, Ontario, Michigan, Erie, and Superior are. . ."

"HOMES!" interrupted Allie.

"What?"

"H-O-M-E-S," added Shoo. "That is how they teach us to remember the names of the five Great Lakes in school. The first initials of all the lakes spell HOMES."

"That's clever," said Mr. Spywell.

"Well, anyway, the combined lakes have about 8,300 miles of shoreline and almost 95,000 square miles of surface area."

Shoo whistled. "Wow, now that's a lot of water."

"It's pretty well-known," remarked their father, "that the Great Lakes have a higher concentration of shipping accidents than any comparable area elsewhere. Unexpected storms are not uncommon on these waters. Ship losses alone number in the thousands. So it's not too hard to believe Mr.

Dimitrius's uncle lost his life in a freak storm sixty years ago."

"Wow, how come they don't teach us about all this in school? I mean about the Triangle in the Great Lakes?" asked Shoo.

"Well, it's not really proven. They have investigated areas along the lakes where **compasses** go crazy. They even think, because of the large mass of **iron ore** located in the **Upper Peninsula**, that possibly a long time ago **meteorites** helped to carve out some of the basins of the Great Lakes."

Allie interrupted, "My teacher said they were made by **glaciers**."

"Well, yes, that is true. But besides that, it could have also been meteorites. We do know that meteorites are masses of iron and at least some scientists think that is why the Upper Peninsula has so much iron ore. In the 1840s both **Douglas Houghton** and **William Burt surveyed** the Upper Peninsula and reported iron ore deposits. Burt said his compass went crazy in the area that is now Negaunee–near Marquette–and that's how he found the rich iron deposits there.

"Now some scientists think there may be magnetic fields under the waters of the Great Lakes that interrupt and play havoc with the equipment on airplanes and ships, and create a strange churning of the waters. Others suggest it might also be caused by underwater earthquakes and the earth's plates shifting."

"Cool!"

"Shoo! That isn't cool, that's scary," protested Allie.

"The world is a mighty big place and we really know so little. It is hard to tell what is going on, exactly."

"Dad, you're a scientist and you're telling me scientists don't know what is going on?" choked Allie.

"I'm an archaeologist, Allie, and what I am saying is that the more I learn and study about things, the more I realize we know very little."

"I agree," said their mother. "I read, study, do research, and travel—yet I am always learning something more. That is why reading and learning is so important."

"I like to read," agreed Allie.

"So if they think all this stuff exists on the Great Lakes, do they think the time **vortex** is real, too?" continued Shoo, "where people can go back and forth in time?"

"Well, let's not get too carried away, Shoo."

"Yeah, Shoo."

"Well, we can't say that it doesn't exist either," argued their father. "How can you explain ghosts? Mr. Dimitrius believes in them. Lots of people claim to see them.

There are many accounts along the Great Lakes of ghost ships appearing to people on a bank of fog. Some claim to have even seen La Salle's ship, the *Griffin*—the one Mr. Dimitrius's uncle named his ship after.

"Really? La Salle's ship?" questioned Shoo. "What about his uncle's boat? I wonder if anyone ever sees that?"

"No telling," said Mr. Spywell.

"So do you think Aunt Diana's house is really haunted?"

"Mr. Dimitrius believes it is, Allie, or was. I've never seen a ghost before, or at least one I've recognized. But it doesn't mean they don't exist."

Allie and Shoo looked at one another and remembered Isle Royale and the ghost of Bloodaxe the Viking. They believed in ghosts. They had even seen one, and it was frightening.

"When I was a girl," added their mother,

"I visited a lot of museums and old houses with your grandmother and grandfather. Every once in a while I would get a chill and the hair on my arms would stick right straight up for no reason."

"Did you get goosebumps, too," asked Allie, "and feel kinda nervous and creepy?"

"Yes, now that you mention it. How did you know?"

"We've seen it on television," interrupted Shoo, as he cast a warning glance at his sister. Allie nodded at Shoo, understanding that it was best their parents did not know about their encounter with the Viking.

The van traveled through town until at last they found the highway. The children caught glimpses of the great glittering lake between the large old mansions which lined the shore. Soon they passed the bluffs that L.T. had spoken about and then the grocery store. A few miles past that was the stand of tall old cedar trees with an isolated road leading towards the lake.

"This must be it," said their father as he turned the van off the main road and followed the pavement until it became hard packed sand.

Great gnarled cedar trees, as tall as any house lined both sides of the road. In some places their roots crept above the sand like fingers coming out of graves. It would have been creepy, thought Allie, if it weren't for the soft sweet smell of the trees. The shadowy path soon opened up onto the flats of a sunny sand dune. Just up the road on a knoll stood two cottages.

"We are here. Look!" Allie said as she pointed.

"Finally," said Shoo.

The first cottage was an old whitewashed clapboard which was weatherworn and nearly stripped of its paint by the force of

the wind. Its shutters, however, still showed a faint shade of green paint.

"That must be L.T.'s place. Mr. Dimitrius, I mean," said Shoo. "It does look like something out of a ghost story."

Diana's cottage was located just beyond Mr. Dimitrius's place. It was painted a soft blue with white window frames and gray-blue shutters. It looked something like a dollhouse. The yard was a mixture of sand and long blowing beach grass. From the sandy knoll they could look down to the beach which was empty for as far as they could see. The lake sparkled, and the cloudless sky above was the color of a bright blue Easter egg. It was beautiful.

There really wasn't a driveway and at first Mr. Spywell was unsure if he should pull up beside the house for fear of sinking into the sand. Slowly he drove off the road and finding the sand to be hard he pulled into the yard. Together the Spywells emerged from the van and started for the door of the cottage. Mrs. Spywell pulled the bright pink key ring out of her purse.

"This place is just perfect. Diana has really done a nice job if this cottage looked anything like Mr. Dimitrius's."

The screen door squeaked open and strained on its spring. Mrs. Spywell fit the key snugly into its hole and turned it. With a click the front door opened into a bright and cheery living room filled with old pictures and antiques.

4

The Cottage

"Wow, this is pretty. Isn't it, Mom?" said Allie as she pushed past her mother and in through the door.

They all agreed.

The four carried in their bags and put them on the floor. The living room had several chairs, a big overstuffed couch, and a long desk filled with books. There were also art magazines everywhere and an easel set up near the window, as their aunt liked to paint.

"I need to use the bathroom," said Shoo who walked to the closest doorway and peeked in. "This is a bedroom."

Allie followed close behind and looked into the same room. It was a small room with bunk beds, a dresser, and lacy window curtains. Allie knew this must be their room. Shoo continued to investigate in search of the bathroom. He walked through a bright yellow and white kitchen and found another bedroom that was much larger, but still no bathroom.

"I sure hope she has a bathroom," he whined. "I've gotta go!"

Mr. and Mrs. Spywell and Allie went to look at the other bedroom. The room was large and sunny with double glass doors that opened onto a deck facing the sand dune.

"This is pleasant," remarked her mother.

Shoo walked back through the kitchen to a door on the opposite side of the room.

"Yeah! I don't have to use an outhouse," he said as he quickly closed the door.

Allie hurried into the living room and picked up her backpack. She knew that she would have to share a bedroom with her brother. If she wanted the top bunk, she would have to move quickly.

Her mother came into the living room behind her. "Will you look at this?" she said as she squatted down and peered into a fireplace. Mr. Spywell came in to see what had drawn his wife's attention. "The fireplace is all set up. Diana even put a **firestarter log** in it so it will be easy to light. All we have to do is touch a match to it and we will have an instant fire in the fireplace. How romantic!" She smiled up at her husband as Allie watched.

Looking around the hearth Mrs. Spywell found a tall tin box, "Here are the matches, too. Diana is so thoughtful."

"That she is. It was sweet of her to let us stay here for the week."

Allie watched and listened to her parents. She didn't get it. It was so warm she couldn't imagine why they would need a fire. And how can a fire be romantic? But she smiled because the fireplace had made her mother happy. Allie walked by her parents on her way to her room as her father stooped down, giving her mother a kiss. Yuck! Allie thought.

In her room Allie tossed her backpack up onto the top bunk and crawled up the wooden ladder at the end of the bed. There, she thought, this is mine.

No sooner did she get settled than Shoo came into the room. "No way, Allie, I found the room first, and I get first call on the top bunk."

"You do not. I'm already up here and so is my backpack."

"I'm tellin'."

"Go ahead."

"Mom, Allie took the bunk I wanted and I saw it first. It's not my fault I had to go to the bathroom."

Allie's mother poked her head into the room. "Yes, you have bunks and there is only one top bunk. Why don't you take turns?"

"Yuck! No way will I sleep in the same sheets he's slept on unless they're washed."

"All right," added their father. "Let's flip a coin to settle it."

Shoo shook his head. "That's not fair. I found the room first." He crossed his arms on his chest and started to pout. "Hey look, here's a couple of coins," he said as he picked one up from the top of the dresser, and quickly flipped it into the air.

"No fair. Let Dad flip the coin," Allie protested.

Shoo missed the catch and the coin dropped on the tile floor between his feet and rolled under the bed.

Shoo dove for the coin as Allie jumped off the end of the bunk, almost knocking her father off his feet. She scrabbled underneath the bed, too, catching her hair in the bedsprings.

"Ow! Help! I'm caught," she screeched.

"Allie, Shoo—get out from under there. What do you think you are doing?"

Shoo slid out on the tile floor and stood up dusting off his shirt. Allie loosened her hair from the bedspring and carefully rose to her knees with tears in her eyes. "That hurt!" she said, rubbing her head.

"You two go sit in the living room with your mother. I'll get the coin."

Allie and Shoo stomped past their father and plopped into chairs as far away from one another as they could be.

"That's it, you two," started their mother, "I've had enough." She stood before them with her arms crossed. "You are guests in this house and you will act like guests. There will be no running, pushing and fighting in here. And take your shoes off at the door. Look. We have already tracked in a ton of sand. And I want you two to stop fighting or we will pack up and go home. Understood?"

Shoo and Allie nodded their heads. Sometimes when they went places with their mother it was really hard. It was more fun, actually, just to go camping with their father where they could run and jump and throw things in the woods.

"I didn't hear anything? Do you two understand?"

Both Allie and Shoo said "yes" in a very polite manner.

From their room the children could hear their father struggling with the bunk beds. He had to pull them out from the wall, since he couldn't find the coin that rolled underneath.

Soon he joined them in the living room.

"I don't know how that coin did it, but it must have bounced and lodged itself into a crack in the wall. I had to fish it out.

"I'm sure glad I did. It is pretty old. It was minted in 1932 during the Depression. It's just one of the many antiques around here. Incidentally, you two will have to be very careful around here."

"Hey, maybe the coin belonged to L.T.," said Shoo.

"Or maybe Uncle Lucas," added Allie.

"It probably did. Look, you two children are not to call Mr. Dimitrius L.T. unless he gives you permission. Remember your manners."

Allie and Shoo both nodded their heads, again.

"Now heads or tails?" called their father.

The children yelled their choices as their father flipped the coin high into the air. He caught it in his hand and covered it with his fingers. As he opened his fist Allie and Shoo looked on intently. "It's heads!" cried Shoo who jumped around in delight.

"That's not fair," said Allie. "I already have my backpack up there."

"It is too fair because I saw the room first." Shoo jumped up from his chair and went into the room with his backpack.

"You better not throw my pack on the floor." Allie jumped up and followed him into the room, pulling the door closed behind her.

"Here," their father rapped on the door, "put this coin back on the dresser with the other one and leave it alone."

Allie's hand flew out through a partly opened door and waved it in the air. Her father dropped the coin into her palm, which quickly disappeared behind the door to their room.

Mr. and Mrs. Spywell looked at one another and shook their heads. "Silence at last."

"Let's check out the kitchen so we can get to the store before it gets late."

Opening up the refrigerator, Mrs. Spywell peered in. "We will need milk, juice, and some eggs."

"We should get the kids some cereal, too," said Mr. Spywell as he peered into the cupboards. He turned on the water faucet and got a drink of water. Checking the other faucet, he realized they had no hot water. "When I get back from the store it looks like I'll have to light the water heater. I bet the furnace, too. Probably both pilot lights are out."

Mrs. Spywell continued to make her mental shopping list, "Cereal, bread, tomatoes, bananas, hot dogs, peanut butter. Okay, I have an idea what we need. We better get going."

Mrs. Spywell walked from the kitchen to the children's room and quietly opened the door, peeking in. She was surprised to see both Allie and Shoo talking nicely from their own bunks. Allie was stretched out on her stomach with a paperback book in her hands and was reading a passage to her brother.

Shoo was lying on his bunk, thumbing through his book, looking at its pictures as his sister read.

"Well, I hate to disturb you," she said as she entered their room, "but we've got to go to the grocery store. It's getting late. Come on."

"Do we have to go? We just got here," objected Shoo. "I'm all settled in."

"What do you mean, do you have to go? Of course, you have to go."

"But Mom," said Allie. "L.T. said—I mean, Mr. Dimitrius said the store was just up the road. We passed it on our way down here, remember? Do we have to go? You let us stay home sometimes when you're making quick trips to the store."

"But we aren't home," insisted their mother.

"Mom, you aren't going to be gone long. And you are just going up the road. Can't we stay, please?"

Overhearing the conversation, Mr. Spywell entered the bedroom. "What's wrong?" he asked. As he asked he glanced over at the dresser to see if Allie had put the old coin back beside the other coin.

"They want to stay here while we go to the store. What do you think?"

"Well, we are just going up to the top of the road, aren't we? We won't be gone more than thirty minutes. Why don't we let them stay?"

"YES!" chimed in the children.

"I don't know. . ."

"Please, Mom? Please. . ."

Mrs. Spywell looked at her children and then she looked at her husband and thought for a moment. "If you two stay, you are not to go outside, and you are to keep the doors locked. Do you understand?"

Allie rolled off her bunk and stood up. "And we are not to open the door to anyone."

"Not to anyone. If we get back and find you have broken any of the rules, I am going to be very upset with you both."

Shoo sat up. "We will be careful, Mom. We promise."

Allie and Shoo looked at one another, delighted by the responsibility their parents had put on them.

"Come on, let's get going. It's getting late."

Allie and Shoo followed their parents to

the door. Their mother turned and disappeared back into her bedroom. "All right. I've checked the doors to the deck from our room and they are locked and the curtains are pulled. Lock the door behind us and stay inside."

As they opened the door Mrs. Spywell realized something had changed outside. The sky was now filled with heavy clouds etched in dark gray.

"Strange, it looks like the weather is changing. That's it, they are coming with us." Their mother stopped in her tracks and turned to the children.

"No!" cried Allie. We will be all right. "It's not going to rain. And besides if it does, you are going to be back before it starts. We are just down the road from the grocery store."

Mr. Spywell looked back up at the sky and at the children. "Come on, let's go.

They will be fine."

"Oh, all right. Lock the door and don't open it to anyone!" she demanded.

"We will," promised Allie. "Bring us back some candy from the store."

Mrs. Spywell smiled at her daughter as she turned and got into the van. They watched as the children closed and locked the door behind them. Allie and Shoo pulled back the curtain from the window and waved good-bye to their parents.

5

CHAPTER

The Storm

Allie noticed her father turn on the head-lights as the van pulled out of the sandy yard. She looked up at the sky. The clouds were gathering. Where each gray cloud bumped into another, it formed a new larger, darker cloud. Maybe it is going to rain, she thought to herself. The van soon disappeared up along the roadway behind the grove of cedar trees.

"Hey, I'm hungry. Let's see what Aunt Diana left us to eat," said Shoo as he ran through the living room to the kitchen. Allie could hear him quickly opening and closing the cupboard doors. By the time she made it to the kitchen, Shoo had his head stuffed into the refrigerator.

"There's nothing here. Nothing good like candy or cookies. There is just asparagus and some jelly. I don't even see peanut butter." Shoo raced across the kitchen and threw open a door to the pantry.

"Are there any crackers?" asked Allie. "We could make jelly crackers."

"Yuck!"

"Hey! Here's a box of raisins." Shoo pulled the box from the shelf and flipped open its top.

"Give me some, too," said Allie. "I like raisins." She reached her hand out and waved it in her brother's face. Shoo pulled away and yanked the box to his chest.

"You want some raisins?" he asked as he pushed his way past her and ran into living room. "Here's your raisin."

Shoo turned quickly and threw one at Allie, hitting her on the side of the face.

"Hey! Cut that out!"

Shoo laughed with delight and then threw another, just barely missing her.

"I said stop it. You will get raisins all over the place and Mom will be upset."

With that, Shoo fired another and another. Quickly Allie bent down and picked up the fruity missiles and took aim back at her brother. Shoo grabbed a pillow to hide behind and kept throwing raisins blindly at Allie.

Allie stormed at him with a handful retrieved from the floor and pelted Shoo as hard as she could. He then plowed over the couch and hid behind it on the floor. All was quiet for a moment until Allie threw herself over the top of couch, grabbing for the box.

Scrambling away, Shoo made for the front door and unlocked it. He flipped the handle and threw the door wide open. Bursting against the screen he strained the spring as far as it would go and let it slam back in Allie's face, just as she went for a tackle.

The two laughed and tumbled out onto the sandy yard. Shoo got up and started to run away just as Allie grabbed for his leg. But as Shoo took flight, he accidentally kicked sand into his sister's face. Allie put her hands to her eyes and howled.

"Ow, ow, ow, my eyes!" Shrieking she spit sand and shook it out of her hair. Then she lowered her head and rubbed her face on her arm.

Running as fast as he could, Shoo raced across the yard and sandy road, heading down the knoll directly to the beach. There the wind blew strongly, and Allie's calls for help were lost in the splashing of waves and the cries of sea gulls.

Allie's eyes burned and watered and the wind kept whipping her hair around her face and into her mouth. She now spit hair and sand at the same time.

"Shoo! Shoo!" she called in frustration.

Along the beach Shoo ran like the wind, racing the waves while being careful not to get his pants wet. His parents would be really upset if. . .if they thought he had gone outside.

Shoo stopped in his tracks and turned around. Allie was nowhere to be seen. Running back up the beach towards the cottage, he could see Allie trying to wobble to her feet and rubbing her eyes. Rushing to her side, he discovered what had happened.

Carefully taking her by the arm Shoo helped Allie to the door. They both pulled off their shoes and tossed them inside. Allie's eyes felt like they were on fire, and she could see nothing through the tears and gritty sand.

"I called to you and you just kept running. You're just such a jerk. Now look what happened. I can't see. I can't see!" she sobbed.

"Hold still, let me see if I can blow the sand out of your eyes." Shoo stood in front of Allie who couldn't even open her eyes.

Quickly understanding that his solution would not work, Shoo offered another. "We better go wash your eyes out," he said, and tugged her through the house, dropping sand from their clothes with each step.

The bathroom was a small, dark room and Shoo couldn't find the light switch. He felt around the wall and under the medicine cabinet, while Allie just stood there with tears running down her sandy cheeks.

"What are you doing?" she demanded.

"I know the light switch has to be here someplace."

"I don't need a light switch. I can't see! Get me to the sink!"

Shoo led her into the dark room and towards the sink. She bent down over the basin while Shoo turned the faucet on. Allie carefully splashed handfuls of cool water over her face, washing the sand out of her burning eyes and soaking her hair.

"I'm sorry. It was an accident," explained Shoo. "It really was."

"I don't care what it was. You shouldn't have gone outside," she bellowed. "You better go clean up that mess in the living room before Mom and Dad get back and find out we were outside and you were throwing raisins."

"You threw raisins, too!" Shoo accused as he left the small bathroom. He knew his sister was right. What if their parents came home right then? He knew they would be mad if they knew what had happened.

Finding a broom in the kitchen corner near the pantry, Shoo quickly swept up their trail of sand and raisins. But since he could not find a dustpan, he swept the mess up under the skirt of the couch where he thought his mother wouldn't look. Suddenly a shadow seemed to pass through the room, and the light in the cabin grew dim. Looking out the open door, he could see the sky was now filled with heavy, dark clouds, and the wind had begun to blow almost fiercely.

Shoo shuddered. It was amazing how quickly the weather could change along the lake, he thought. Closing the door behind him, he turned on a lamp. As he inspected the floor, he found another raisin which had escaped his broom. He picked it up and popped it into his mouth. It wasn't too sandy, he thought as he crunched down onto the grit.

Returning the broom to the kitchen he watched Allie in the dim bathroom as she continued to wash out her eyes. He did feel sorry for what had happened, but after all, he thought, it was an accident. Just then he noticed a light switch on the outside of the bathroom wall. When he flipped it, the light in the bathroom glared brightly from the ceiling.

"There it is, on the outside of the bathroom. That's odd."

"Shoo, this really hurts." Allie straightened up, her hair dripping wet, her face and eyes swollen. She cautiously opened her eyes and peered into the mirror above the sink. Her eyes were bloodshot, her cheeks beet red. "Mom is going to know we went outside. She is going to know what happened. I'm going to have to tell her. You are in so much trouble, Shoo. Did you clean up the mess in the living room?"

Shoo nodded his head. "She won't know. Just put a cold washcloth on your face and sit down. The swelling will go down."

From outside there came a sound like the low rumbling of a car engine.

"They're home! They're early! Shoo, did you lock the front door again?"

Shoo dashed into the living room and locked the door. At that instant another rumble was heard, this time rattling the cottage. A shot of lightning lit the dark sky that lay between the surface of the lake and below the black clouds. Shoo jumped. It wasn't his parents, it was a storm.

Somewhat relieved, Shoo pulled back the window curtain and watched the clouds roll.

"Hey Allie, it isn't Mom and Dad," he called. "It's just a storm." Shoo walked through the cottage to find his sister's swollen face staring back at him from the bathroom mirror.

"You better get a cold washcloth on that

before. . ."

"Look at me! Look at me! I'm a mess. My eyes are all swollen."

"Here, let me get you a washcloth," insisted Shoo as he pushed his way past his sister and opened the linen cabinet in the bathroom. It contained piles of neatly folded washcloths and towels.

"I don't need your help! Just get out of the bathroom," she snarled.

"But I. . ."

"Get out! You're such a jerk!" Allie grabbed Shoo by the shirt and threw him out the door, slamming it shut in his face.

"I only wanted to tell you Mom and Dad aren't home yet, but it is going to storm." Another long rolling rumble of thunder filled the air. "Did you hear that?"

Allie blindly felt around in the linen cabinet and found a washcloth, ignoring her brother's words. She took it to the basin and soaked it with cold water. She squeezed out the excess water from the cloth, tilted her head back, and placed it over her eyes, pressing gently. She removed the cloth and was still looking up at the ceiling when the light clicked off.

Outside she could hear Shoo laughing loudly. "There, how's that for being a jerk?"

"Shoo, you turn that light on!"

There was silence. "Shoo, turn that light on!" she screamed from the black room. Still there was silence. She reeled around and began to turn the doorknob. Instantly the light flicked back on. He better not do that again, she thought to herself.

Picking up the washcloth, Allie again held it to her sore, swollen eyes. But as soon as she got the cloth to her face, the lights went out again. Allie pulled the cloth from her face. Shoo was going to get it now! She grabbed the doorknob, giving it a yank. The door wouldn't budge.

Using all her strength she pulled and budged it open slightly before it slammed shut again. "Shoo, you are going to be so sorry when I get out of here."

She tried turning the doorknob, but Shoo held it tightly from the other side. Allie was getting angrier by the second. "Shoo, turn the light on and let me out!"

"Not until you say you're sorry for calling me a jerk," he demanded. At that instant, a roll of thunder shook the cottage, startling Shoo just enough that he loosened his grip on the door handle.

Allie threw the door open and chased him into the living room, swatting and stinging him with her wet washcloth each time she got near him.

Shoo turned to stand his ground and reached out for Allie as a bolt of lightning lit up the sky outside. With a sharp crack its electricity exploded just outside the cottage. Both children jumped with fright. Forgetting their argument, they ran to the window and jerked back the curtain, looking to see if the lightening had hit anything. Outside the wind now blew harder and they could see headlights coming up the road.

"They're home! It's Mom and Dad." Allie ran to the bathroom and flipped on the light, closing the door behind her. She tidied her face as best she could and pulled her damp hair around her ears. Maybe she could just stay in the bathroom for awhile. She could take a shower, she thought.

Shoo watched out the window. The lights on the road came closer and then vanished. Where did they go? Where were his parents? wondered Shoo.

As the wind picked up more speed it made the old cottage groan. Shoo continued to look out the window, searching for the headlights that had disappeared. As he watched, the lights in the cottage dimmed, once, twice, and on the third time, went out entirely. He stood alone in the dark room as a storm started to rage outside.

From the bathroom Shoo could hear Allie yelling at him to turn the lights back on. She is never going to believe this, he thought.

The house was now entirely dark and Shoo could feel the temperature change as the air began to cool. There was an eerie dampness all around him. Slowly he made his way through the dark cottage. Allie had stopped yelling at him, and the house was silent except for the storm. Shoo felt his way along the wall and just as he reached the kitchen, he ran into Allie who was making her way out to him.

"What did you do to the lights? Mom and Dad are going to be so mad at you.

What did you do?"

"I didn't do anything. I think it's the storm."

"I don't know where Mom and Dad are. I saw their headlights, but then they disappeared."

"What do you mean they disappeared?" she snapped. "I wish they would get back so I can tell them what you've done."

Allie pulled back the window curtain in the living room and stared outside. Puffs of fog blew in on the wind like ghostly pieces of cotton candy. Shoo joined her at the window, watching the storm as it approached. Soon rain started dropping from the sky. First, big splats hit the windowpane. Then the rain pelted down, hitting the window so hard it seemed as if it was trying to force its way through the glass. The cottage felt creepy and lonesome.

"Hey," said Shoo. "I think I saw a flashlight in the pantry on the shelf when I got the raisins." Shoo felt his way along the wall past the stove towards the pantry. He opened the cabinet and ran his hand along a shelf.

"I found it! It's here," he said joyfully pulling the flashlight out and flicking the switch. A faint round beam of light cut through the darkness.

"Finally you've done something right," Allie sneered. She scrunched up her face as Shoo shined the light into her red swollen eyes.

"Knock it off!"

Outside the wind started to howl and whistle around the corners of the house. Shoo cast the light away from his sister's eyes, and they both stood silent at the frightening sound.

"What's that?" asked Allie. She could feel goosebumps run up and down her arms.

"I don't know, but I sure hope it's not a ghost," added Shoo.

6

Visitors

The little cottage shook as walls of wind slammed against its frame. Allie and Shoo had been in many storms before, but this one was different. It seemed almost alive.

Outside a great bolt of lightning reached out its twisted fingers across the sky and again lit the clouds from underneath. Shoo and Allie jumped at the sudden flash and raced back to the living room window. Pushing the curtain aside, Shoo leaned forward and pressed his face against the cool glass, staring out towards the shore. "Did you see that? The whole sky lit up. This is wild."

As Shoo stared out, his breath steamed up the windowpane. "Hey! Look Allie. . .

that's strange."

"What? What is it? Let me look." Allie pushed her way in beside her brother.

"What did you see?"

"I don't know, but it looked like. . .." Shoo took his hand and wiped the steam off the glass. "It looked like someone was down there on the beach walking." He pressed his face to the window again.

"I don't see anyone. What would anyone be doing out there in a storm? It's a mess out there." Allie shoved her face closer to her brother's, and two rings of steam quickly formed on the glass in front of them. Allie moved so she could see better. There—walking on the beach—there was someone!

"Move!" shouted Shoo as he quickly wiped off the glass again. "There. Look! Can you see?" They both could plainly see the dark form of a person. It looked like a man wearing a long cape. He held his arms up high over his head and was shouting towards the wild, churning lake.

"Who is that? What's he doing?"

Allie shivered and pulled away from the window. "Is the door locked?" she asked. Quickly she ran to the door and checked the handle by giving it a quick turn. It was locked.

"Look now!" cried Shoo. "What's that?" Allie pushed against Shoo to see. "It looks like there's a ship or something out there with lights on the front of it. Something with big sails heading right towards shore!"

Outside the thunder rumbled so loudly that it sounded like the pounding of great guns.

Allie pushed herself closer to the window and saw a ship riding in front of a dense bank of fog. Its sails were billowing and straining against the force of the wind. She could see two small lights near the **bow**.

"The storm, the storm is going to blow the ship onto shore," exclaimed Allie. "Why are the sails up? Why are the sails up in a storm? That's stupid."

The children watched as the man on the beach shook his arms wildly in the air, screaming out to the mad wind. He ran back-and-forth along the shore.

"Should we go out and help?" asked Shoo. "Maybe we can help."

"Shoo, shine your flashlight out towards the water. Maybe the ship will see it's close to land."

The two ran to the front door, unlocking and opening it. The wind and rain blew in on them through the screen. They shined the dim light, waving it wildly towards the rolling sea. The children jumped up and down yelling as loud as they could, hoping to help the endangered ship, but their voices were lost in the wind.

The water now glowed as if there was a light shining up from beneath the pounding waves. As the ship drew dangerously close to shore, the wind pulled feverishly at its sails and with one final blast, stripped the sails from the **rigging**. The ship moaned. It was going down. Allie and Shoo watched in horror as the great arms of the **mast** tumbled forward and fell onto the **deck**. The two lights glowed eerily out in the wild waves.

Allie screamed and Shoo held his breath as the great bank of fog following the ship closed in around it, swallowing it up. The two lights faded as the ship disappeared from sight.

The shadowy form of the caped man on the shore turned directly towards the children. Their light, no longer waving, shined out towards the figure on the stormy beach.

The figure was silent and didn't move. Although the children could not see his face, they could sense the man's sadness. Then, just like the ship, he disappeared into the bank of fog.

Shoo lowered the flashlight and looked over at his sister who stared blankly towards the beach. Quickly she grabbed Shoo and pushed him aside, slamming the door shut and locking it behind them. Together they leaned against the door and wondered what they had just witnessed.

Shoo was the first to move and he walked back to the window. Outside the house was now engulfed in the fog. It was a blanket of white so thick, nothing could escape.

Shoo stood with the flashlight and waved it over and over again to see if anything happened. But the fog only reflected the light back into the cottage and lit the dark room.

Allie went over to the couch and slowly sat down. She was wet from the rain blowing in through the screen. Where were her parents? What happened to the ship? Who was that man?

Shoo turned to her and shined his flashlight into her eyes. "Cut it out," she demanded. Then she added "We better get a towel and dry the floor."

"Yeah," agreed Shoo. "Come with me to get the towel. Allie? What happened out there? You don't think that was a ghost we saw, do you?"

"Come on, let's get that towel." Allie didn't want to talk about it. She didn't know what it was, but she was sure they would have to wait until the fog cleared to find out.

"I hope Mom and Dad are all right," said Shoo. "You think they are all right? They wouldn't be able to drive in fog like this. I hope they stayed at the store."

Allie nodded her head. They had to be all right. The two walked through the dark house with the help of the dim light of the flashlight. They found their way to the bathroom, and Allie carefully pulled out a large bath towel while Shoo stood nearby.

"This will have to do," she said as they made their way back through the kitchen to the living room. Allie stooped down and carefully wiped up the rain from the floor. The wind outside continued to whistle eerily around the corners of the house. Shoo could feel the cool dampness right to his bones, but there was something else. He smelled fish!

"Do you smell that?" he whispered.

Allie stood and sniffed the air. It was getting colder and she shivered. "I can't smell anything, but I am ice cold." Allie took the towel and folded it. "Let's try to turn on the heat."

Shoo shined the light along the wall until he spied a thermostat. Allie stood on her tiptoes and carefully moved the dial, listening for the furnace to light. There was no sound.

"I didn't hear anything, did you?" She moved the dial again. Nothing.

"I guess the furnace doesn't work," added Shoo grimly.

"Give me the flashlight. I'll get our sweatshirts out of the backpacks."

Shoo sniffed the air again. He was sure he could smell the stinky smell of gutted fish. It was everywhere. "Do you smell anything, Allie?"

Allie sniffed a couple of times and crossed her arms around her. "No. I'm just cold. Give me the light."

"You aren't going to leave me out here alone in the dark. I'll go with you." The two carefully made their way into the bed-room. Locating their packs they found their crumpled shirts and pulled them over their heads. They were warm and soft. That was better.

As Allie pulled her hair away from her eyes she thought she could see a shadow moving back and forth outside the little window of the bedroom. Quickly, she grabbed the flashlight from Shoo and switched it off.

"Hey!" protested Shoo.

Allie reached out and clamped her hand over his mouth and whispered for him to look. As they stared at the window, a dark shadow flickered across the lacy curtain. There, back-and-forth, back-and-forth, the shape moved. It looked like a man— maybe the man from the beach.

"Who is it?" whispered Shoo.

"I don't know." They watched the

shadow move as if suspended in mid-air. They were both petrified. Allie, gathering all her courage, slowly walked towards the window and reached out to push the curtain aside. Just then they heard a long low moan coming from outside the cottage. The two froze, barely able to breathe.

Allie, feeling the hair on her arms standing tall, scooted up next to the wall with Shoo right beside her. Ever so slowly she pulled back the corner of the curtain. Bringing her nose as close to the window as she could without being seen by the mysterious form, she peeked out.

At that very instant, something big and bright yellow flapped hard against the window. Allie jumped back and screamed, falling against Shoo who tripped and fell onto the floor. Shoo yelled as Allie came tumbling down hard on top of him, the flashlight escaping his grasp and rolling across the cold tile floor.

"What was that? What was that?" shouted Shoo as the two tried to untangle themselves in the dark. "Where's the flashlight?" Allie panicked. They both felt around the cold floor until Allie finally touched the cylinder which had rolled under the edge of the bed.

Frightened, the two sat on the floor with their backs to the bed. Allie flicked on the flashlight switch. It wouldn't go on. She clicked it again. It still wouldn't go on. Shoo grabbed the flashlight from her and shook it as hard as he could until a faint ring of light glowed from it. With a little light and renewed courage, Allie stood up and carefully pulled the window curtains wide apart. Plastered against the glass was a yellow rain **slicker**, suspended from a wooden hanger on a clothesline attached to the outside of the house. Allie and Shoo were quiet for a moment, and then they both burst into laughter.

"Aunt Diana must have forgotten to bring it in from the clothesline. I'm surprised it hasn't blown all the way to the grocery store by now." Allie was embarrassed by her fear, but relieved.

"Yeah, she must have forgotten it," agreed Shoo who took a deep breath and smiled at his sister. As the two stood before the window their flashlight began to grow dimmer and dimmer. Shoo held it still, not wanting it to go out. But the light flickered a little and then all was black.

"Oh, no. . .. Give me that." Allie took the flashlight from Shoo's hand. "I don't believe this." She shook the light again and again. Through the curtain, they could see lights outlining the form of the yellow rain slicker.

"It must be Mom and Dad coming

back." They were both relieved. "Let's go sit in the living room and wait." The two carefully made their way to the living room. This time Allie, too, could smell the stink of fish. She was glad it was too dark for her brother to see her face and discover how frightened she was.

They sat silently, side-by-side in the stinking room waiting for their parents to open the door. It seemed like an eternity in the cold, dark, creepy cottage. Finally Shoo stood and went to the window to look out. There was no van. No Mom or Dad. "There's no one there."

"Didn't we just see lights? Didn't we just see them?" asked Alllie. "Shoo, do you smell. . .?"

"Fish? Yes, I smell the fish. I guess those haint blue shutters of Aunt Diana's don't work too well."

"Shoo, this isn't funny."

Shoo stood before the window and looked out. The fog had thinned considerably. It now appeared like the film on the side of an empty milk glass. The wind had also died down, but the thunder rumbled like a drum to remind them that the storm was still around. Occasionally, long flashes of lightning streaked across the sky, making the children jump.

Lowering the curtain Shoo went back to the couch and sat silently with Allie, listening to the storm and smelling the smell of fish.

"Hey!" said Allie softly, breaking the silence. "The fireplace."

"What about the fireplace?" asked Shoo.

"Aunt Diana laid the wood for a fire. Don't you remember? When we first got here? Mom and Dad were talking about it."

"No. And you better leave the fireplace alone."

"You must have been in the bathroom. Aunt Diana had the fire all ready to start. Mom said there was even a firestarter log in there. All we would have to do was put a match to it."

"I don't know, Allie." Shoo hesitated. "Do you have matches?"

"We have matches. They're in a tin box, someplace over there beside the fireplace. Mom found them earlier."

"Allie, I don't think we better mess with the fireplace."

" Shoo, this is an emergency. We don't have any lights. We are cold. The place smells like dead haunted fish. And the fire is ready to be lit.

"We've started fires lots of times when we were out camping with Dad. I think we have to."

Allie slid off the couch and onto all fours to the cold floor. Carefully she made her way across the room to the hearth, where she felt around for the tin box of matches. There, just to the left of the mouth of the fireplace, was the box. Being careful not to drop the box in the dark, she lifted the lid, reached her fingers in and pulling out a long match. She felt the lid for the sandpaper strip to light it with, but there was none.

"I can't believe this. How can we light a match?"

Shoo slipped off the couch and felt his way to Allie's side. "Let me see."

"No, you dingbat, neither one of us can see." Allie started to giggle a bit in her nervousness as she tried to make a joke.

"This isn't funny. You know what I mean." Shoo reached out and felt for the box. When Allie was sure he had it, she passed it over, still holding onto the match.

Shoo ran his hand over the tin. Finally he found the strip of sandpaper near the bottom. "I found it!"

Allie reached out her hand with the match while Shoo held the box tight. She placed the tip of the match along the strip and slowly drew it across. The match didn't light.

"You've got to do it fast," said Shoo.

Allie again found the rough spot and this time, with a flick of her wrist, snapped the match across. Instantly a tiny blaze of light appeared. Its white and orange flame made them both see floating circles. Allie held the match by its long tail and slowly moved it towards the fireplace. She touched the flame to the paper end of the starter log and watched as the paper caught. Allie tossed the match into the fireplace and watched as the paper began to flare. But within seconds the paper crumpled into black ashes while the sparks died away to tiny pinpricks of light.

"We're going to need another one," said Allie.

"No kidding." Shoo opened the lid of the box and reached in for another. "Let me do it this time," he insisted.

"No. You hold the box still and I'll strike it." Allie found the match in the dark, pulled it from her brother's hand, and yanked it across the sandpaper. Again it flamed. Taking the mini-torch to the starter log, she held it still until it caught and burned brightly.

Shoo took the matches and laid them away from the fireplace. Allie stood and jumped up and down. "I did it! Let there be light!"

"And heat," added Shoo.

They could smell the burning paper and the waxy starter log and then the dried wood itself took the flame. Shoo sat close to the fire, hoping to warm up and dry out.

At least the smell of the fire masks the smell of the fish, he thought. He smiled as the bright flames from the fireplace filled the room with light. But soon, his eyes began to water.

"Shoo, do you smell smoke?" Allie's eyes which had just recently recovered from the sand, began to water again. "Shoo?"

Shoo stood up away from the fire and wiped the tears from his face. "Maybe it's just. . .."

"Shoo, there's smoke in here." Allie started to cough. "We better get the door open."

Shoo made for the door, unlocked it and yanked it open. As he did the screen door behind it suddenly opened as well, and the door frame was filled with the dark silhouette of a man.

7

The Rest of the Story

Shoo hollered loudly, slammed the door shut, and leaned hard against it. "There's someone out there," he yelled. "Help me!"

The door rattled against his back. It was being forced inward by the shadowy form outside. Allie dove for the door, trying to help her brother. If only she could lock it, she thought as she pushed with all her might. Gray smoke from the fireplace now filled the room. They began to cough in spasms.

"Hey, you two!" shouted a cranky sounding voice from outside. "Let me in. What's a-matter with you?"

"Who is it?" coughed Allie.

"It's me, L.T. Let me in. What's wrong

with you?"

Quickly Allie and Shoo opened the door and let old Mr. Dimitrius come in from the rain and fog. Shoo took the door and began swinging it back-and-forth to help clear the smoke.

"What's going on in here? What have you been up to?" The old man began to cough.

"We tried to light a fire in the fireplace. The lights went out and there was something out on the beach and…"

Mr. Dimitrius flew across the smoke-filled room to the fireplace and quickly reached up inside its chimney. "Well, for crying out loud, you two didn't open the **damper**." With a quick yank on the lever, the children watched as the flames stood straight up and the smoke was pulled from the room up into the chimney.

"Close the door. Let the damper do its

work," he bellowed at them.

Shoo, realizing the screen door was still open and banging in the wind, pulled it shut. Then he closed the door and locked it tight behind him. The old man coughed and coughed and cleared his throat.

"What in tar-nation are you children doing here alone? Where are your folks?"

"They just went up to the store. They were only going to be gone for a few minutes."

"Yeah, I bet that was before the storm hit though, wasn't it?"

Shoo and Allie nodded their heads. "Would you please go get me a drink of water, young lady? My throat is all dried out with that smoke." The old man coughed and coughed. The room began to clear, leaving a smoky smell behind.

Allie made her way into the kitchen as the fireplace glowed and its warm flames lit the room. She brought Mr. Dimitrius his water. He stood before the flames in his yellow rubber rain slicker and yellow boots and gulped the water.

"You two sure gave me a fright, darn near scared the life out of me at that door," he said, wiping his stubbled chin with his hand. "I was just getting ready to knock.

"I thought I best come over here and check things out. I was over to my place when the storm hit."

"Those must have been your headlights we saw coming up the road," said Shoo.

"Yeah, probably. About the time I got up in the attic at my place to check out those squirrels, I heard the wind pick up. Before I could get myself down off the ladder the rain was already coming in. Then that big bolt of lightening hit. Did you see it? Hit over into the trees. Didn't know how bad it was, though, until I tried to leave."

Allie and Shoo looked at the old man and wondered what he meant.

"Did it hit something?" questioned Shoo.

"Did it hit something? It sure did. I was on my way out of here in my truck when I got to the top of the hill and there was one of those great big old ancient cedars blocking the way. The whole road was covered with tree. So I came back down here to the cabin and called the city and reported the tree down."

"You have a phone?" Allie asked excitedly. "Maybe we can call the store to tell our parents we're all right."

"I had a phone. It was just about that time the lights and the phone both went dead. Only thing we can do now is wait until the storm blows itself out or the city moves that tree. Whichever comes first."

Allie paused for a moment. She knew her

parents would be panicked.

"I bet your folks are waiting at the end of the road right now for the workmen to get that tree out of the way."

"Yeah, maybe we could walk up there and. . ."

"Walk? What? Walk up there? What's a-matter with you, boy? There's an electrical storm going on out there. You aren't goin' no place. Don't you have a flashlight?"

"We did have but it went out," said Allie.

"Went out, did it? Maybe I can fix it. Let me get this wet gear off and warm up a bit."

Mr. Dimitrius removed his yellow slicker, sat down in the chair beside the fireplace, and tugged his boots off. On his feet he wore mismatched socks with holes in the toes. "Well, lookie there. My toes have popped through. Must be time for a new pair. Got me a matching set of these floating around the house someplace," he said with a chuckle and wiggled his toes in front of the fire.

Allie took his yellow rubber coat and hung it over the back of a chair to dry. Shoo took his boots and put them near the door, at the same time straightening their own shoes which they had taken off before the storm. The old man leaned forward in the chair, casting his shadow into the room and pulling his blue sweater tightly around him. Shoo was glad he was there.

"Mr. Dimitrius?" asked Allie.

"I'm Lucas Thomas or L.T. Mr. Dimitrius is my father," said the old man with a smile.

Allie smiled at him, "Lucas Thomas. L.T., did you see anyone out on the beach before you came in?"

"Yeah," added Shoo. "Someone wearing a cape?"

"A cape, you say?" asked the old man. "No, I didn't see anyone out there when I came over."

"So there wasn't a ship or anything? A ship with two lights that just kind of disappeared in the fog?"

L.T. looked up at Shoo and over to Allie. "So you've seen a ship, have you? A ship with sails and two lights?" Both the children nodded their heads.

"Why, I'll be. You've seen it then. . .."

"Seen what?" questioned Shoo.

Allie looked at their guest. What was he talking about?

"This is gonna call for a cup of tea, I'd say. I'm chilled to my old bones." L.T. scooted forward in the chair and stood slowly. "And let me take a look at that light."

"I don't think there is any hot water. I don't think the stove works either," said

Allie as she handed the flashlight to L.T.

"Well, I am sure your Aunt Diana has a tea kettle and we have a nice warm fire, so we can put it right in there to boil up."

"Yeah, just like camping," said Shoo as he jumped around in delight. "I'm really glad you came over, L.T."

"Me too," Allie agreed.

L.T. smiled as he worked on the flashlight. It had been a long time since he had been needed by anyone.

The flashlight once again in working order, L.T. made his way to the kitchen where the children were hopelessly trying to find a tea kettle. "Now you kids stand back so I can shine this light in there. Allie and Shoo moved back near the pantry shelf so L.T. could see.

"Well, now, there's a bunch of pots and pans in there but no kettle. Never heard of anyone without a kettle before. I'm stumped."

"Maybe it's in the pantry," said Shoo as he opened up the door and felt around.

"Here, let me see." The children stood aside in the doorway of their parent's bedroom while the old man shined the light across the shelf.

"Not much here, except. . ." he paused for a second, "except this." L.T. pulled a plastic bag of something out of the pantry. Let's make this instead of tea."

"Son, Shoo, that's your name, right?"

"Yeah, Shoo."

"You look over there in the oven for a pan with a lid. Here–" he turned towards Allie.

"Allie's my name."

"Sure strange names your folks picked for you two. Here, Allie, hold onto this." L.T. put a plastic bag full of round pellets into her hand and returned to search the pantry shelves until he found a tall, slender plastic bottle. "That'll do it. Did you find a pan with a lid that fits tight?"

"I think so," answered Shoo.

"Let's get back to the fire."

With their mysterious treasures the three made their way back into the living room and L.T. sat down in the chair. "Put the pan between my feet," he instructed.

Shoo leaned down and put the pan and lid between L.T.'s mismatched socks.

"What's this?" asked L.T. as he picked up a raisin near his foot and held it up to the light of the fireplace.

Allie and Shoo started giggling, having forgotten all about their raisin fight.

"That's mine," said Shoo. "Looks like I lost one." Allie gave her brother a dirty look and Shoo started to laugh at their secret.

Allie held the bag of yellow pellets up to the light. "Hey, it's a bag of popcorn without the microwave bag. Don't we need a microwave for this?"

"You modern kids, don't know nothin' about making things the right way. You never had good popcorn until you have it over an open fire.

"We've had it over an open fire before when we went camping with Dad," said Shoo. "It was in one of those tin pans with the foil over it, like you get in the store."

"Well, this is the old-fashioned way of making it.

L.T. unscrewed the lid of the slender oil bottle and poured in just enough oil to cover the bottom of the pan. "Now give me the corn." The old man poured a pile of corn kernels in the pan and swirled them around until they were covered with oil.

"Where's the lid." Shoo pointed down to L.T.'s feet. "There we have it. Now get back and let me down there. My old bones don't move like they used to.

I sat here many a night with my mother years ago, making popcorn just like this. Haven't done it in years, though. Kind of brings back memories."

L.T. carefully rose from the chair and eased himself down on his knees by the fire.

"Get me one of those cushions off the couch. Don't remember the floor being so hard as this."

Allie removed one of the cushions from the couch and L.T. set it on the floor as far back from the fire as he could for safety. Sitting on the edge of the cushion he pulled his sweater around him and pushed up its sleeves. Then he put the pan out over the flames and started swirling it around.

"There we go. Got to let the oil get hot. If the weather weren't so bad I'd hike up into the woods and look for some leeks for us. Cut those up in hot oil and make it up

with your popcorn. Tastes like a cross between garlic and onion. Can't beat it." The
old man grinned up at the children.

"L.T.?" said Shoo. "I don't think those
blue-colored shutters keep ghosts out very
well."

"Is that right?" said the old man staring
up at Shoo. "Now, why do you say that?"

"Well, right before you came and before
the fireplace got smoky, Allie and I could
smell fish. It stunk really bad. You know,
like fish blood and guts."

"Is that so?" L.T. looked back into the
flames and set the pan down into the ashes.
He rubbed his hands together and looked
out into the shadows at the children.

"He's right," said Allie, nodding her
head.

"Did you two happen to see a couple old
coins floating around here?" asked L.T.

Shoo's eyes grew wide with fright. "What

do you mean, floating?"

"Not floating, floating—lying around on a table or a dresser," snapped L.T., jarring Shoo back from his image of hovering coins.

"The coins. . ." blurted Allie. "Yes, there are two old coins on the bedroom dresser in our room. Why?"

"Well, then, there ain't nothin' to fear from old Uncle Lucas." L.T. stared back into the flames of the fireplace.

"Why do you say that? What do the coins have to do with anything? asked Allie.

"Those coins, those are 'safe-keeping' coins. When an old salt, a sailor, didn't return home from the sea, the family would always keep two coins near at hand. Coins for the dead man's eyes—to keep the lids shut and to keep the sailor from haunting their loved ones. If Diana kept those old coins I gave her, it can't be Uncle Lucas that's up to mischief in this house."

Allie and Shoo moved closer to the fire. Allie thought about the old coins in their room and how they had flipped one to see who would get the top bunk. Coins for a dead man's eyes, she thought. It made her skin crawl.

"Did I hear you two say you saw both a man down at the beach and a ship?"

"Yes, a big ship," added Allie.

"A big ship with sails blowin' hard before the wind? Could you see lights shining from its bow?" questioned L.T.

"Yes! That's the one." Allie and Shoo nodded in agreement.

"Well, I'll be. Anything strange about the man on the beach?"

"Not really, just that he was out in the rain, and he had a cape on. We could see it blowing in the wind."

"That's it? Did ya hear any singing and chanting, any voices calling from the lake?"

Allie and Shoo's eyes grew big.

"Any guns firing off or bells ringing?"

Allie and Shoo shook their heads. "No, but the thunder and wind were so loud it would have been hard to tell.

"What did we see? Who was the man?" questioned Allie.

"Let me tell you something, children. What you witnessed tonight was pretty special. I've lived around these parts all my life, and I've heard story after story of the same thing—just what you two saw tonight. But never in my life have I ever been privileged to see it myself."

The oil in the pan started to sizzle and they heard the first ping of a popped kernel hitting the lid of the pan.

"Here we go," said L.T. as he reached over and grabbed the handle of the pan. "Owie, that's hot. Allie, get me something so I don't burn my hand."

Allie made her way into the kitchen, but was not able to find a potholder. Then she ran into the dark bathroom and grabbed a couple of washcloths and folded them together. In the living room she handed them to L.T. who quickly made a mitt out of the cloths and lifted the pan from the ashes. The corn kernels popped one at a time, first slowly and finally exploding with sounds of excitement as he swirled the pan. The smell of the hot oily corn filled the air and made them all hungry.

"Sure smells better than fish and smoke," said Shoo with a laugh.

"Shoo, where'd ya get that name?" asked L.T. with a smile as he worked the pan over the fire.

"It's. . .."

"It's short for Sherlock," interrupted Allie. "Like Sherlock Holmes, my mother's favorite detective."

"Allie!" snapped Shoo. "Well, Allie gets her name from Alexandria, Egypt, where our father was working on a dig when she was born. My mom's a writer and she likes detective stories. Sherlock Holmes is her favorite."

"Those are good names. They have stories behind them. You two should use those names instead of Allie and Shoo. They just sound funny." L.T. laughed to himself.

"So tell us more about the man and the ship," urged Shoo.

"Just one minute, Sherlock, wait until the popcorn is finished. I'll tell you, Sherlock. Yes, I like that name. Sherlock."

Allie started giggling. "Alexandria, you don't think you can find me some butter in that fridge, can you?" he asked.

Allie looked seriously at L.T. No one else except her grandmother and her mother (when she was mad) called her that.

Shoo started laughing. "Alexandria. . .."

"Be quiet, Sherlock," she snorted as she passed by into the kitchen. When she returned she brought a tub of butter and a spoon.

"This is all there was, I don't think it's really butter, but it is supposed to taste like it."

"Well, that will have to do. Thank you, Alexandria. Now come over here and sit down and I'll tell you the rest of the story. The two children drew near as L.T. shook the pot, holding onto its lid, until the corn stopped dancing. Carefully he slid the pan out of the fireplace and opened up the lid. The popcorn steamed and the smell filled the room. L.T. scooped out large spoonfuls of the soft yellow cream from the butter tub and swirled it around the inside of steaming hot lid. It melted into a soupy mess. "There we are. Now here's the trick," he said as he held onto the handle of the pan and quickly flipped the lid over it, letting the soft oozing liquid melt down over the white flowery popcorn. Then he took the pan and shook it as hard as he could. "Got to get it all coated," he said as he pulled off the lid. The steaming white popcorn was now yellow.

"I know where the salt is," said Shoo as he jumped up and ran to the dim kitchen. He returned with a shaker and sprinkled it over the contents of the pan.

"Popcorn anyone?" asked L.T. who grabbed a handful of popcorn first and tossed a few kernels into his mouth. "Mmmm, can't beat that now, can you? That fake butter isn't too bad, either," he said with a satisfied smile. L.T. and the children stuffed their mouths with popcorn.

Shoo smiled and was glad they were all together. He threw a piece of popcorn at his sister, bouncing it off her head.

"You don't want to be wasting food with silliness," L.T. said to Shoo. Allie looked at Shoo and scrunched up her face with a smile.

8
CHAPTER

LaSalle and the Griffin

"Now, for the story. Do you two believe in things you can't explain? Like another world mostly hidden from us, like shadows in the fog or mysterious smells?" L.T. looked up at the children and waited for their response. Allie and Shoo looked at one another and nodded slowly.

"It's like the wind that blows and howls. We can't see it, but we know it's there. We can feel it on our skin, yet it's invisible.

"I don't believe there is any one reason why ghosts appear or ships return, time and time again, only to repeat their tragedy with groaning timbers and crying men. But some say they do.

"Some say those downed ships travel forever at the bottom of the lakes, doing the jobs they were made for. Lamps all lit, men working the lines.

"Well, I believe there's something to all that hubbub. That is why this story ain't for the faint-hearted."

The children scooted closer to L.T. and the fire. Allie felt icy tingles up and down her spine.

"That ship, that ghost ship you two spied out there on the lake, rushing to its doom. I sure wish I had seen it. They say, if you look carefully at that ship, you'll see the eyes of its **figurehead**, a **griffin**, glowing out at you, aiming for its destiny."

"We saw lights out in front of the ship— two of them, didn't we Allie?" whispered Shoo. Allie nodded. Goosebumps danced up and down her arms.

"What's a figurehead?" asked Shoo.

"I know what a figurehead is," commented Allie, "but what is a griffin?"

"A figurehead is the mascot, the eyes of the ship. They say a ship will be continually lost without its eyes. La Salle chose the figurehead of a griffin for his ship. Carved by the hands of craftsmen in France, fashioned after the emblem on Frontenac's, his boss's, coat of arms. Frontenac was the Governor of New France and godson of King **Louis the XIV** at the time La Salle and the *Griffin* sailed the Great Lakes. Stories say that figurehead brought with it a curse from France as they hauled it across the great salt sea, yanked it up the cliffs of the Niagara and carried it on the backs of men into the wilderness.

"Those that have seen the ghost ship say the eyes of that figurehead, the griffin, burn through the fog and paralyzes with fear anyone that sees it. You two are lucky to be here to be able to tell your story," said L.T.

"What does a griffin look like?" asked Allie.

"A griffin has an eagle's head and wings and a lion's body. It's a frightful looking thing."

Shoo gulped, "Do you think we saw the ghost ship *Griffin*?"

L.T. stared into the fire as he munched on his popcorn. "It sure sounds that way to me."

"The *Griffin*? La Salle's ship, the *Griffin*?" said Allie in amazement.

"That's the one. And that man you saw, the one with the cape, it might just have been the ghost of Rene Robert Cavalier, Sieur de la Salle, himself. They say he walks the beaches of the Great Lakes dressed in a scarlet cloak edged in gold, the one he wore while he was still alive. He's searching for his lost ship. Most of his appearances are right before a big storm."

"Why does he do that? Why does he keep looking for a ship that sank over three hundred years ago?" questioned Allie.

"Don't know. No one knows. I believe he was a determined and stubborn man. He built the first sailing vessel to ever get to this part of the Great Lakes. The Indians called it the Great White Bird, but to La Salle, it was really a floating fortress.

"Some say he keeps coming back, calling to the lake to return what rightfully belongs to him. Calling the *Griffin*. Some say they have heard the voices of Frenchmen chanting their prayers, begging La Salle to let them go to their rest, to return to their watery grave to do their work.

"They also say the ghostly form of the ship has been sighted all around the Great Lakes. Around the coast of Lake Michigan, from Green Bay to Mackinac. Some even say they have seen her on the Huron in

Georgian Bay, on Lake Superior and even Lake Erie."

"What happened to the *Griffin*?" asked Allie.

"I bet it got caught in the Great Lakes Triangle and is in a time warp. That's what happened to it. Just like La Salle. That's why they keep coming back."

"What?" asked L.T. "What are you talking about? A time warp?" L.T. shook his head.

"Shoo, be quiet. Let L.T. talk."

"How do you know so much about La Salle?" asked Shoo.

"Well, I don't know so much. But I sure did study about La Salle when I was a lad, especially after my Uncle Lucas was gone. I figured it kind of made me close to my uncle since he named his boat after the *Griffin*. And when I was out on the lake with my uncle, he used to talk about La Salle

140

and that ghost ship. I think my uncle kind of admired La Salle's determination and his stubbornness. My uncle was like La Salle, a man who would never give up."

Allie watched L.T.'s wrinkled face as he munched on his popcorn and gazed into the fire, remembering the past. She was surprised how smart he was and by his uncle's efforts to teach him history when he was young. Uncle Lucas sounded a lot like her parents.

"Wow, that's cool," added Shoo. "So tell us about La Salle and what happened."

"Well, in 1679, La Salle had that ship *Griffin* built around Niagara area, close to what is now Buffalo, New York. He had his men carry all the riggings and anchor, and that figurehead around the falls and down the other side. They built that ship in the wilderness with the Indians watching them. Some even helped.

"When they finished they launched it into Lake Erie, the first sailing ship on these Great Lakes. La Salle planned to follow the route set down in 1673 by the Jesuit priest named **Marquette** and an explorer named **Jolliet**."

"I know about Father Marquette and Jolliet. We studied about them in school. They were the first Europeans to discover the Mississippi," added Allie.

"Those are the two," agreed L.T. "Well, La Salle had no idea just how far he was going to have to go to find that route, but he had the general directions right. He sailed across Lake Erie, turned into the straits of Wa-we-a-tu-nong, or Detroit, and up into Lake St. Clair where he sailed even farther north against the current on into Lake Huron. All along the way he and his crew fought storm after storm. It was terrible. The journey was full of danger from the start.

"They went north and paid a visit to Marquette's mission site where St. Ignace is today. Then they went on to the Baye des Puans or what's now **Green Bay**, Wisconsin. There they loaded the *Griffin* with furs to help pay for the expedition. La Salle's plan was to leave the ship at this point and take a small expedition of fourteen men to the mouth of the Miami River here at St. Joseph and build a fort. His captain was to take the *Griffin*, loaded with furs back to Niagara, cash them in and bring back supplies to build another ship on the Mississippi River.

"The records left by Father Hennepin, the priest on the expedition, said the *Griffin* dropped La Salle off at Green Bay in August of 1679. He also said they loaded tons of furs on the ship and that they were even tanning deer hides off the sides of the boat. The boat literally hung with furs.

"La Salle, on his own with only fourteen men, made his way down along the lake and up around until he reached the Miami River, here at St. Joe. He built his fort up near the place we met this morning and waited for the *Griffin* to arrive.

"From there, he and his men were all supposed to travel along the Miami to the Kankakee in Indiana to the Illinois River to the Mississippi. There he planned to build a new ship so he could sail the Mississippi."

"Can you imagine building a ship by hand in the wilderness?" interrupted Allie. "A big ship at that. He was really determined, wasn't he?"

L.T. continued. "La Salle staked all he had on that great enterprise. I suppose that is why he is still waiting and watching the waterways, calling the *Griffin* to join him."

"If the ship never returned, did he ever make it to the Mississippi?" asked Shoo.

"He sure did. He claimed the entire Mississippi River region in the name of his king, Louis the XIV, in 1682."

"But what happened to the *Griffin* and La Salle?" asked Allie

"I'm getting to that," smiled L.T. as he took another handful of popcorn and crunched on it kernel by kernel. "By the time La Salle built that fort it was almost winter and the weedy edges of the river were getting glassy with ice. The *Griffin* still hadn't returned. La Salle stayed here as long as he could. He even sent men back up to St. Ignace to wait and send word if the *Griffin* arrived there. When the weather started to get cold, he and his men moved southwest, down along the Illinois River to winter with the *Iliniwek* or Illinois Indians. He built another fort down there called Fort

Heartbreak. I guess 'cause he was broken hearted about losing the *Griffin*. There's still a town over there in Illinois where that fort was built, still carrying that name."

"A town called Heartbreak?" asked Allie.

"Well it's a little fancier than that, its called Creve Coeur. That means heartbreak in French. It's across the river from Peoria. Been there a couple times myself.

"No one knows for sure what happened to the *Griffin*."

"But what about La Salle? Why does he keep coming back?"

"Well, Sherlock, I think it's because he had so set his heart on that ship. It was so important to him that he just can't let it go. He's still waiting, calling the *Griffin*, waiting for its return.

"La Salle himself returned to Canada. Walked all the way across southern Michigan. He even went back to France for a while, but when he returned, he came back with three ships and sailed them to the Gulf of Mexico where he was looking to enter the Mississippi from the Gulf. In Texas a group of men mutinied and one of those nasty rascals shot La Salle and left him to the elements."

Allie and Shoo looked at one another. "His own men killed him?" asked Allie.

"That's what history tells us."

"Wow! That's really mean. He was an explorer."

"Yep, those people that first came here to this new land, opening up this nation of ours, they had a real hard time of it. They gave everything they had, including their lives for exploration. This country was as new to them as outer space is to us now."

"Wow," said Shoo. "Just think where we might be in space in just three hundred years."

"Or maybe in the ocean," added Allie. "We don't know much about the ocean either."

"It's all enough to make your head spin, to think about it," commented L.T. with a smile.

Allie sat nibbling on her popcorn and staring into the glowing fire, thinking about all that had been said. There were lots of sad stories from the lakes, thought Allie. She looked up at the old man, his face outlined in the glowing fire. He certainly knew a lot of history and it was nice to have him here, she thought.

Shoo watched as L.T. picked unpopped corn kernels from the pan and tossed them, one at a time, into the fire. "I wish Mom and Dad were here. I hope they are all right," he said.

"They're fine, son. They'll be here straight away. Don't you worry about them.

As soon as the city gets that old cedar tree pulled aside, they'll be coming down that road. The city is pretty good at keepin' this road cleared. I told them I was stranded down here, so I am sure it won't be any time at all.

"I guess you could say we're the lucky ones—sitting here inside with a nice warm fire and some popcorn. Then there are the ghosts waiting just outside the door, calling to us, hoping to be remembered with a story. Did you two really smell fish in here earlier?"

"Yes," said Shoo nodding his head. "It really stunk. Like fish guts."

"It really did, L.T. It really did," agreed Allie.

"Just don't get it with those dead man's coins still here. . .." L.T. sat back on his cushion, his wrinkled old face frowning as he popped some more popcorn into his mouth. "It's been a long time since I've smelled that smell in this house. I bet my mother's old rockin' chair is rockin' away all by itself over at my place, too. Sometimes ghosts are comforting. Sure wish I would have smelled that old fish smell again."

"Yuck!" said Allie. "It stunk!"

L.T. grinned and chuckled. "I miss my old Uncle Lucas Thomas. He was a good man. He was a good man to my mother and me when we needed him. I never did stop looking for that red cap of his."

L.T. chewed on his popcorn and watched the scarlet flames licking at the wood.

CHAPTER

The Gift

Shoo got up and went into the kitchen and then to the dark bathroom. He wished his parents were there to hear L.T.'s stories He was sure they would have liked them.

On his way back to the living room Shoo turned on the faucet and let the water run until it was nice and cold. He filled three glasses from the cupboard, balanced them in his hands, and carried them to the fire. Outside a drum of thunder sounded overhead as Shoo handed out the glasses.

"Why, thank you, Sherlock. I'm not used to havin' anyone wait on me. I kind of like it." L.T. smiled up at Shoo.

Allie took her glass and slowly swallowed a mouthful of the cool water. "Thanks

Sherlock," she said teasingly.

"No problem, Alexandria," he responded.

Shoo took his water to the window and tugged back the curtain to look out at the dark shore. The rain now fell gently against the windowpane. The fog had moved out across the lake and looked like a layer of snow on the black water.

As Shoo's eyes adjusted to the dark, he searched the shore for any movement. For a moment he thought he saw something. He watched closely as he took another swallow from his glass.

There it was again.

Shoo went to the front door. Unlocking it he peered out towards the shoreline. Softly glowing in the dark was the figure of the caped man. Now someone else was standing next to him. They both stood facing the lake, looking out over the water, La

Salle's cape catching and blowing in the wind.

"Hey, you guys. You're not going to believe this, but I think he's back, and he's brought a friend."

Allie's eyes opened wide. She looked at L.T. who stopped chewing his popcorn. A glowing ball of light appeared on the porch, just on the other side of the screen door.

"Help me up!" exclaimed L.T. "Quickly! Help me up, children. This, I have got to see." Shoo helped Allie pull L.T. to his feet. Stiffly L.T. straightened out his legs and shook out his pantlegs, hobbling as fast as he could to the open door. The ball of light faded away as they drew near the door.

Together the three of them stood in the doorway starring out into the darkness. A cool breeze carried raindrops gently through the screen and onto them. As their eyes adjusted to the darkness, they saw two forms, glowing with a soft, hazy glow. They were on the beach just down the hill from the house.

"I see them. I think I see them," whispered L.T. "By everlasting George, there they are. As plain as day."

They watched as the two figures slowly floated up the knoll until they were almost straight across from the door of the cottage. As they drew near, the three could see a bright scarlet cape flowing from what they thought to be the shoulders of the great explorer, La Salle.

"If that's La Salle," whispered Shoo, "who is the other one?"

"He wasn't here before," added Allie quietly as they all watched.

"No, it was just the one guy with the cape. They weren't glowing before either."

The three stood watching as the forms stopped, once more, and looked out across the great lake. There was no more lightning or thunder—only the pounding of the waves against the shore and the gentle rain.

L.T. watched in disbelief, shaking his head in amazement. "Never in all my days did I ever think I'd see something like this."

They watched as the caped figure's light started to dim and he gently floated out over the lake. Slowly, slowly the glow faded until it was no more.

The other form remained on the beach, looking at the lake, until the glow had completely disappeared. Then it slowly turned and faced the cottage. It lifted a softly glowing arm and pulled something from off its head, waving it in the air.

L.T.'s breath caught in his throat as the face of the man, lit by its dim glow, came into view. In his hand was a bright red cap. Tears streamed down L.T.'s cheeks as the figure waved the cap towards the cottage

once again.

Forgetting himself, L.T. raised his arm and waved back. "Why, I'll be." Tears rolled down his cheeks as he smiled into the dark. Allie and Shoo encircled L.T. with their arms as they watched the ghostly form walk down the beach and fade into the night.

L.T. was so shocked and happy that a grin covered his wrinkly face from ear to ear.

"L.T., are you all right?" asked Allie.

"Am I all right? Why I am better than all right. That was Uncle Lucas, and he's all right, too." L.T. wiped his nose on the back of his hand and laughed out loud.

"Look!" pointed Shoo. Coming down the road were headlights, real headlights on a real automobile. As it drew nearer, they could see it was the van.

"You two better get this room picked up before your parents raise a fuss about the mess," instructed L.T.

Allie quickly grabbed the couch cushion and shoved it back in its spot. Shoo picked up the glasses and oil and took them out to the kitchen. Allie followed with the pan of popcorn and the salt shaker. L.T. was just putting his hankie back in his pocket as Mr. and Mrs. Spywell came in the door.

"Oh, you just won't believe what happened," exclaimed Mrs. Spywell as she came in the door with a bag of groceries. "Are you two all right? Oh, Mr. Dimitrius, I'm so glad you're here. I was worried. There was a tree fallen across the road and the city trucks were out there working in the rain, trying to get it pulled away. It was a mess." She crossed into the kitchen and returned.

Mr. Spywell entered carrying two more bags of groceries. "Thank goodness you're here, Mr. Dimitrius. I was about ready to hike down the road, if we were going to have to wait much longer."

"Well, folks, it's been my pleasure," said L.T. as he coughed a little and cleared his throat. "I was out workin' at my cottage and thought I'd stop by for a visit. The children and I have just been sitting here next to the fire eating popcorn and swapping stories."

Allie's Mom and Dad smiled at one another. "See," said Mr. Spywell to his wife.

Then he turned to the children. "I told your mother you were safer here at the cottage where nothing was going on than if you were with us. It was a real mess up there for a while. We were worried when we couldn't get down to you."

All of a sudden a snap of electricity ran through the wires of the cottage and the lights blinked on.

"Hey, they fixed the lights, too. Everything will be fine now," said Mrs. Spywell.

"Yep, everything is fine now," repeated

L.T. who looked down at the children and smiled.

"Well, I guess I'll just skedaddle back home," said L.T. as he slipped on his boots and pulled on his yellow slicker over his sweater.

"Be careful going back into town. There were still a few branches down in the road."

"Oh, I'm not going into town. I'm going home to the cottage, maybe rock in the old rocking chair for a while. That's as good a place as any to lay my head."

Shoo opened the cottage door and Allie held open the screen. "Hope we see you tomorrow," said Allie.

"Hey, what are these?" Allie leaned down, peering at the porch floor just outside the screen door.

"They're coins," said Shoo as he pushed in for a look. "They look really old."

"I think these are for me," said L.T. as

he squatted down and picked them up. He held them gently in his fingers, turning them one at a time, to the light. Squinting, he read the dates to himself.

"Why, I'll be. . . .. They're old all right. They were minted the year I was born." L.T. looked at the children, the crinkly skin gathered high around his eyes as he smiled at them sadly and walked away into the darkness.

They watched as L.T. left and walked across the yard towards his cottage. He stood for a moment and looked out over the lake. Finally he turned, realizing the children were still watching, and lifted his arm in a wave good-bye.

Glossary

archaeologist. A scientist who studies past lives and civilizations through material remains.

bow/prow. The front of a boat or a ship.

Burt, William. A well-known government land surveyor who is remembered for discovering iron ore in Michigan. He also invented a solar compass.

carcass. The dead body of an animal.

compass. An instrument for determining direction with a needle that points to the magnetic north.

damper. A moveable metal plate that regulates the flow of air to a fire in a fireplace.

deck. Any of the horizontal floors in a ship.

depression. A long period of inactivity of business or trade; specifically, the Great Depression during which up to 17 million people were unemployed.

figurehead. A carved image at the prow or front of the ship.

firestarter log. A commercial product of pressed wood fibers and wax used to help start fires.

Fort Miami. Fort located along the Miami River (St. Joseph River, Michigan), built by the explorer La Salle and his men. The fort was built in 1679 and was known to be in existence until 1688.

Frontenac. Second Governor of New France (France's land claims in North America) and godson of Louis the XIV.

fur depot. A location used during the fur trade to collect and store furs. The first forts of the Great Lakes were created as fur depots to protect the precious merchandise.

Georgian Bay. A huge inlet of Lake Huron in Canada.

glacier. A massive block of slow-moving ice.

Green Bay. A large inlet on Lake Michigan in the state of Wisconsin.

Griffin. The first sailing vessel to sail in the upper Great Lakes, built in 1679 by LaSalle and his men.

griffin. A fabled creature having the head and wings of an eagle and the body of a lion.

haint blue. The color of a blue or green paint pigment mixed with buttermilk, used primarily in the southern United States by those who are superstitious and wish to keep ghosts from their homes.

Houghton, Douglass. An important surveyor in Michigan whose discoveries and work led to the beginning of the state's copper and iron mining industries.

iron ore. Rock containing iron which was an important natural resource in Michigan's Upper Peninsula. Iron mining spurred the settlement of the U.P.

Iroquois. A group Indian tribes related by language and culture who formed a powerful confederacy. Although they lived in the eastern Great Lakes region, they tried to control the fur trade in the western Great Lakes area as well.

lookout. A place from which to observe who might be approaching.

Jolliet, Louis. French explorer and trader who traveled with Father Marquette along the Mississippi (four months) in 1673, covering over 2,500 miles. First known explorer, with Father Marquette, to travel the Illinois Country.

Louis the XIV. King of France who laid claim

to all the territory in North America traversed by French explorers, missionaries and traders, and asserted supremacy over all Indian tribes of those areas.

Marquette, Jacques. Jesuit priest who was first known explorer of the Illinois Country (1673). He also established a mission at St. Ignace in what is now Michigan's U. P.

mascot. A person or thing believed to bring good luck.

mast. A spar or structure rising from a boat which holds the sails and rigging.

meteorite. A fragment of rock or metal reaching Earth's surface from outer space.

Northwest Passage. A fictitious passage once thought to lead across North America to the Orient.

oilskins. Rain gear made with a strong fabric treated with oil for waterproofing.

Oumiamis/Miami. An Algonquin-speaking tribal group that once lived in the southwest corner of what is now Michigan.

rigging/lines. Ropes to support the mast of a ship and work the sails.

skiff. A small light boat.

slicker. A raincoat.

survey. To determine the exact shape, boundaries and position of a piece of land.

Upper Peninsula. The northern part of Michigan between Lake Superior, Lake Michigan, and Lake Huron.

vortex. A whirling mass of water or air with a visible column.

whirlpool. A current of water whirling in the center and drawing objects into it.